M000215472

AVOIDING ALPHA

AILEEN ERIN

First Published in 2014 by Ink Monster, LLC
Ink Monster, LLC
34 Chandler Place
Newton, MA 02464
www.inkmonster.net

ISBN 9780989405065

For my love, Jeremy.

You inspire me every day.
Thank you for sharing your life with me.
I can't do it without you.

Chapter One

A pillow hit my face. I shoved it under my head. "What?"

Meredith plopped down on my bed next to me. "You're seriously telling me that Hotty McHottypants is in your room nearly every night and nothing ever happens? How is that possible?"

I rolled my eyes at her use of 'Hotty McHottypants' for Dastien, my mate. She'd been on a kick the past week, trying to find out about us. The thing was, he'd been a perfect gentleman. "He's furry when he sneaks in. I swear."

Meredith groaned. "Really? Every time?"

I cross my heart. "Yup. Why do you think my sheets are so hairy?"

"Maybe because you needed to improve your hygiene practices?"

I snatched a pillow and slammed it into her face. "My hygiene is perfect, thank you very much." I tucked my legs under my covers, and Meredith took that as an invitation to get in bed with me. We were both in our PJ's—tank tops and shorts. I'd already gotten ready for bed—my teeth were freshly brushed and face was squeaky clean. It was Tuesday night and we had class early in the morning, but Meredith liked to chat a little before bed. Sometimes being at St. Ailbe's Academy—a secret boarding school for werewolves—felt like one long sleepover. It was nice, especially since I hadn't had a sleepover in...ever.

I grabbed the latest Nora Roberts masterpiece from my nightstand, while Meredith started to flip through this month's *People Stylewatch*.

"I still say there's more going on between you two," she said after a few minutes. "You're just being shy about sharing the juicy details."

"I wish." I blew out a breath. "He's been going on patrol most nights, and keeps saying that he's waiting for the whole full moon thingymajig before heating things up too much."

"Thingymajig? Thingymajig! The Full Moon Ceremony is more than a thingymajig."

The way she said the words—like they seeped importance—made my stomach knot. "Uh. Don't remind me." Until seven-ish weeks ago, I'd been a plain old half-*bruja*, aka Mexican witch, with visions. Whenever I touched things—a person, a T-shirt, even just a light brush against a wall—I saw whatever was the strongest emotional memory in that object. But Dastien bit me and now I was some sort of werewolf-*bruja* mash-up. I was still in the figuring-it-out stage, but the werewolf part gave me control over my visions.

The Full Moon Ceremony was supposed to cement me and Dastien's mate bond. Make it unbreakable. So, it was normal to be nervous about it. At least I hoped it was normal…

"The Ceremony's on Saturday. A mere four sleeps away. Are you ready for it?" Meredith asked.

God. I didn't know *how* to be ready for it. Going furry still made me incredibly nervous.

Sweeping the topic under the carpet was probably a bad idea, but I couldn't help myself. Avoidance, deflection, and repression were my BFFs lately. And I couldn't forget about handy, dandy redirection. "So, how's Donovan?"

She turned the page on her magazine so quickly the page tore. "How should I know?" Her words didn't mask her scent—a hint of citrus meant that my question made her anxious.

Donovan Murray was one of the Seven—the group of Alphas who rule all werewolves—and he totally had the hots for Meredith. "Please. I know there's something going on with you two. And it rhymes with shmates."

I poked her side and she slapped my hand away. "There's nothing going on. There won't be. I'm cursed, and that's just all there is to it. No shmates here. And, by the way, that's a horrible rhyme. It's not even a word."

That's why Meredith was avoiding Donovan? Because of some stupid curse?

She had a run in with the local *bruja* coven three years ago and hadn't been able to shift since then, but the curse hadn't caused any adverse affects for her. At least none that she had mentioned.

If Meredith was turning down Donovan because of the curse, that definitely counted as an adverse affect.

I put my book down and rolled onto my side to face her. "You guys would be a good match. Maybe even a true mated pair."

She didn't say anything, but the magazine crinkled under her grip.

Okay, so maybe I needed a different approach. "It's obvious that he likes you. Those looks he sends your way…" I fanned myself.

"Shut up." She hit me with her magazine.

"Your violence only helps prove my point."

She turned the page, this time more gently. "I don't want to talk about it."

Here we go again. She always made me talk about things that I didn't want to, but when the time came for her to spill, she didn't. The girl was a closed book.

"Do you think Dastien is going to come by tonight?" She asked, changing the subject right back to what I didn't want to talk about.

I went easy on her and let the Donovan topic go for now, but I wasn't forgetting about it. "Probably." I thought about Dastien. His dark hair, amber eyes, and wicked smile. The little bit of cockiness to it, plus the sincerity and dimples…it melted me every damned time. The past few weeks, we'd grown closer, moving beyond our initial attraction. It'd been a little all consuming at first, but beyond that, we had a lot of the same interests. Books. Music. Dancing. And no one could make me laugh like he did.

I hoped he'd come by tonight.

"Well, just remember protection."

I gasped. "Meredith!" Why was she bringing this up now?

"I'm being serious. I'm not ready to be an auntie yet."

My cheeks were burning. "We're so not even there yet." Thank God I had the latest DJ Tiesto mix playing from my laptop. I didn't want anyone overhearing this conversation. Werewolves' ears were extremely sensitive.

"But you have to swear to spill when you do." She put the magazine down and grinned at me.

"Oh my God." I put my hand over her mouth. "Stop before someone hears," I whisper shouted at her.

Meredith reached across me for my laptop remote on my nightstand, turning up the volume. "The Full Moon Ceremony is as good as a wedding. We should talk about what you're going to do after, if you know what I mean." She waggled her eyebrows at me.

"Shut up." I leaned back on my pillow and closed my eyes. "I'm nervous. About it all. Shifting. Being with him. Am I supposed to live in the dorms still? I know he's got a cabin somewhere on campus, but I haven't been there yet. Plus, I'm turning eighteen the same day. That's entirely way too young to be married. It all seems so weird and I feel awkward bringing it up with him. I don't really know what to say."

"Just talk to him. He'll understand."

"I don't know. I think bringing it up might hurt his feelings, but taking such a huge step right now is crazy...but then I think about Dastien, and maybe it's not so crazy. But that could be the hormones talking." I groaned. "I've lost my mind. I'm rambling. Say something, please. Make me feel better about this whole thing."

"You haven't lost your mind," a low gravelly voice said beside me.

I squealed and opened my eyes. Dastien was crouched beside my bed, his eyes level with mine. "Oh my God. How long were you listening?"

"Right as she was advising you on taking precautions."

I hit Meredith. "You knew he was there, didn't you?" I threw the covers over my head as they started to laugh.

"You both suck and I hate you."

Dastien pulled the covers down a little. His smile was big, showing his dimples. "*Je t'aime, cherie.*"

God. He just killed me with that look. And then telling me that he loved me in French…

He leaned forward, pressing a soft kiss to my lips.

"That's my cue to leave, but think about what I asked." Meredith stood, but stumbled on her first step.

I leapt across the bed. Thanks to my quick werewolf reflexes, I caught her before she hit the ground. "What was that?"

Meredith looked a little pale. "I don't know. The room spun. That usually only happens on the full moon days."

This was so not good. Werewolves were graceful at all times. They never tripped, stumbled, or got sick. I pushed her back on my bed. "Sit." I grabbed a Coke from my mini fridge. "Drink this. Maybe you're hungry?" Whenever my wolf was getting control, I felt a little out of sorts. Food usually helped.

Meredith downed the drink, and I looked over at Dastien. "Is this normal?"

He shook his head. "None of what Meredith has gone through is normal."

"If you talk about me like I'm not here, I'm going to flip out," Meredith said.

Ignoring her, I pulled out a chilled Snickers bar from my mini fridge. "Eat." Her color looked a little better once she was done. "How do you feel now?"

"Fine. I get a little off around the full moon. Must have started a little early this month or something. Nothing to worry about."

I looked to Dastien as he crossed his arms, mouth pressed in a firm line. Still he gave a tiny nod, telling me it was okay but that he was worried. I was worried, too.

Even if she got this way during the full moon, I didn't like it. Adrian—the only Were here who also had *brujo* blood—had mentioned trying to figure out a way to break the curse before, but I'd gotten caught up in all the vampy-werewolfish stuff. It was time for me to be as good a friend to Meredith as she'd been to me.

She stood and I held my arms out, ready to catch her if she fell again. She slapped them away. "Chill. I'm fine."

"If you say so." But I still watched her as she walked away, ready to jump into action.

"I say so." She went through the bathroom that joined our two rooms together. "See you in the AM." She closed the door to my room and the water turned on.

I turned off the music on my laptop and climbed back in my bed.

Dastien toed off his shoes. He was still fully clothed in jeans and a plain gray T-shirt.

"You think she'll be okay?" I asked as he slid under the covers with me.

"*Oui.*" He opened his arms, so I settled down with my head on his chest. "Weres don't get dizzy, but she does on full moon days. It's a little early for that, but she could be having an off day. Things have been tense around here."

He wasn't joking. Vampires had invaded campus my first week at St. Ailbe's. My second week, Dastien, Mr. Dawson—the principal—and a few others had gotten kidnapped as part of a werewolf coup. Since then, the pack had been a little stressed. It was slowly getting better, but it'd taken a toll on everyone.

He ran his fingers through my hair. "I'm sure she'll be okay once the moon passes."

"She'd better be," I said.

"I'm heading out to patrol, but I wanted to come say goodnight before I left." The campus had been on lockdown every night since the vampires had shown up on campus. They hadn't come back so far, but he spent at least part of every evening making sure no vampires came back.

"Okay," I said, but I really wanted him to stay.

"But then I heard what you two were talking about..."

I scrunched my eyes shut. This was so embarrassing.

"We have to do the Full Moon Ceremony this month, *cherie*. I know you're scared about changing and what the ceremony means, but the Tribunal starts next Wednesday. If we don't do it now, our case won't be as strong. I have to do everything in my power to make sure you're safe and that we have a future together."

Dastien had broken werewolf law number one when he bit me. He'd lost control. Usually that meant death, but since we were true mates, Donovan and Sebastian—two of the Seven—pardoned us. Unfortunately, I lost control shortly after that and nearly ripped out Dastien's ex-girlfriend's neck, which brought up the issues all over again. Imogene deserved it, but her father still filed a complaint against us, calling for a formal Tribunal. Nothing could stop that once the process started.

Next week, the Seven and a bunch of other pack alphas would come to St. Ailbe's to decide our punishment. Everyone kept saying it would be okay, but Dastien was right. We needed every little thing we could get to help our case.

I knew in my head and in my heart that doing the Full Moon Ceremony was the right move, but I was still nervous. "So, what comes after the ceremony?"

Dastien pressed a kiss to the top of my head. "That's entirely up to you. I'm not rushing you on anything else. I think I've done that enough."

I sat up enough to look at him. "I wouldn't have it any other way." I meant that. I really, truly loved Dastien.

As our mate-bond settled in, we grew more in tune with each other. Meredith swore that after we did the Full Moon Ceremony silent conversation over any distance would be just as easy as actually talking. Until then, we could only feel the other's strong emotions.

His love burned hot through our bond as he held me.

Someone knocked on my door, shouting something in French.

"That's my cue," Dastien said.

"Are you coming back tonight?"

His frown made his left dimple show up. "We're hunting the far grounds. It'll be really late before I get back, and you need your sleep. Dr. Mozan's test is tomorrow, right?"

I nodded.

"Good luck. I'll see you tomorrow at lunch, okay?"

"Okay. Stay safe."

"Always, *cherie*." He got up, pressing another soft kiss against my lips. "Want me to get the light?"

"Please." I curled up against the pillow. It smelled like forest and something just him. Closing my eyes, I let go of the worry, and sunk into a deep, dreamless sleep.

Chapter Two

The sound of metal and plastic shattering against the wall startled me from my sleep.

"Again? That's the third one you've broken this week!" I yelled to Meredith. Both doors to our connecting bathroom were open, so I could see straight through from my room to hers. "Tell that alarm clock how you really feel."

"It needed to go to hell. So I sent it there." Meredith's voice was muffled, still mostly asleep. "I'm freaking tired. Need more sleep."

For a girl who was positively perky all the time, Meredith moved slower than molasses when she first woke up. Everyday it was the same. She'd hit her snooze at least five times. Every once in a while, she'd chuck the alarm clock against the wall in frustration. But three days in a row was a streak, even for a girl who stashed boxes of them in her closet.

Rolling out of bed, I grabbed a fresh towel, and went to shower. Once I was up and dressed, Meredith usually got going.

The bathroom's tiny black and white hexagonal tiles were cold beneath my feet. I pushed the shower curtain aside, and turned the water on, and then closed the door to Meredith's room.

Bathrooms used to be a nightmare for me. Before, wearing gloves was the only way to stop from getting visions. Unfortunately, gloves had never panned out in the shower. Total nightmare. But now I didn't need the gloves. Without visions hitting me all the time, I got ready so much faster.

I opened Meredith's door when I was done. Her room was a riot of color. She had endless make-up and beauty supplies in the bookcase next to her bed, and a desk piled with magazines. She was still completely covered by her comforter. I poked where I thought her back might be. "Your turn." She grunted, and I went back through the bathroom to my room.

The layout was a mirror image of Meredith's, but where Meredith had color, I had white. Mostly because I had to make sure that everything I touched was brand new and extra clean. Bleach helped burn the visions out of anything. It wasn't necessary anymore, but it'd become a habit.

Three long metal shelves were drilled into the wall beside my bed. They held actual books, in alphabetical order by author and sorted by genre. The framed print hanging above my bed was knocked askew. Underneath a big grinning Cheshire Cat, in big purple and pink block letters, it read, "Keep calm. We're all mad here." It'd been a gift from my brother. He was enjoying college life, but I missed the dork.

I quickly dressed in skinny jeans and a T-shirt, and

checked my watch. I was actually making good time this morning. I might even have time to review my notes on Dr. Mozan's chemistry class before breakfast.

I paused as I brushed my hair. Why wasn't Meredith in the shower yet? She was always up by now. "Hey? Are you getting up?"

She didn't answer.

I went through the bathroom and into her room. She was still huddled under her covers. "Come on, chica. It's time to get up. You're gonna miss breakfast." She didn't respond at all. "Hey, you okay?" I pulled the blankets away from her face.

Meredith blinked her bloodshot eyes at me. A piece of her hot pink hair was stuck to her forehead. "I don't know. My limbs ache."

Aching limbs sounded like the flu. "You seem sick, but that's—"

"Impossible," Meredith said. "Werewolves can't get sick."

That might be true, but she looked pretty pale to me. I pressed the back of my hand to her forehead. "You're ice cold." Which was odd. All over Texas it was hitting over ninety degrees, and werewolves ran hotter than humans.

"I'm not sick." She sat up. "I'm just feeling extra slow today. It's a side effect of the curse. I'll be fine once I'm up and about."

I raised my eyebrows, but said nothing. She'd know better than me what was wrong with her. "Well, I'm going to finish getting ready. You gonna get up?"

"Yeah. Today's French toast day. I'm not missing that for anything. Just give me ten, I'll be ready."

"Cool." I went back to my room and shoved my homework in my Tokidoki messenger bag. Meredith closed my door to the bathroom and turned on the shower. I opened my laptop to go over my notes, but a message from my brother, Axel, was in my inbox. The subject line read, "Whasrt'ds uopl?"

Was that English?

I snorted as I opened it. It took a bit of deciphering, but I got the gist—he went to a party last night. The send time said three AM. Poor guy would be hurting when he woke up. I turned on the latest from BBC Radio One's Essential Mix—a totally sweet set from Sasha and Pete Tong at a club in Manchester—and started replying to Axel's email.

I was about to hit send when the smell hit me. I paused the music.

"Meredith?" I asked through the door.

She gagged, and my blood went cold. Meredith hadn't been lying when she said that werewolves didn't get sick. They could heal broken bones in a few hours.

So, why was Meredith puking in our bathroom?

My chest tightened. Something was seriously wrong with my best friend.

I knocked on the bathroom door. "You okay in there?"

More noises followed that I wished I hadn't heard. Especially not with my new super sensitive hearing. Yuck.

I took a deep breath and fully cursed my werewolf senses. I could smell her half-digested food—the fried pork chops weren't so appealing on the way out. There was something metallic in the air, too. Willing myself not to barf, I cracked open the door.

Meredith's hair blocked her face from my view as she hovered over the toilet. I glanced around the bathroom, trying to figure out what I could do to help as she heaved. The mirrored medicine cabinet didn't have anything even remotely medicine-like in it. Werewolves didn't need it.

What was I even looking for?

Right. Hair band. I searched one of my carefully organized drawers beneath the sink, not caring that I was messing it up, and grabbed a black elastic. I quickly tied her hair back.

A chill ripped through me. "Umm…Meredith? Is there blood in your puke?"

"What the hell is happening to me?" Her voice was soft, and shook with fear. "I've never been sick like this before. I've never thrown up in my life. During the day of the full moon I get weak, but not this…"

"I don't know what's going on." I pressed the back of my hand to her forehead. It was still clammy. "I'm gonna get help."

Before I got to my cell, it was ringing. Dastien's photo lit up my screen.

"Hey," he said as soon as I answered. I could hear the leaves crunching under his feet as he ran. "What's wrong? Why are you panicking?" He'd no doubt felt my freak out through our bond. My fear for Meredith definitely qualified as a strong emotion.

"Meredith's puking blood."

"*Merde.* Watch her. If she starts seizing, call me back. I'm grabbing Dr. Gonzales on my way."

"What do you mean if she starts seizing? What the hell's going on?"

The line was silent. He'd hung up?

Shit. He'd totally hung up on me.

Seizing? I ran through the little bit of first aid training I was forced to do in health class back in Los Angeles. Move them away from anything that could hurt them. Cushion their head. Loosen constrictive clothing around their neck.

Meredith was curled up on her side, hopefully done with puking. She was far enough away from the tub that she probably wouldn't hit her head.

Her clothing—a hot pink tank top that matched the dyed sections in her hair and a pair of black sleep shorts—wasn't constrictive at all. I grabbed a towel from our rack and folded it to put under her head.

"I feel horrible," Meredith said. I ran a washcloth under hot water and handed it to her. She wiped her face before quickly sitting up, barely making it back to the toilet as she dry heaved.

"Take slow, deep breaths. It might help." I sat on the edge of the tub next to her, rubbing my hand up and down her back.

She closed her eyes, following my advice. "Have you ever puked before?"

"Uh, yeah. I used to be human."

She started puking again. If possible, Meredith turned even paler. I tried not to look—I didn't want to—but it was like a train wreck. I couldn't turn away as a little bit of blood dribbled from her mouth.

"How do you get used to it?" She said when she got back under control.

I snorted. Meredith had grown up a Were and had never been sick before. I was the only wolf in a very long while to be turned from a human. "No one gets used to it. Throwing up sucks." It especially sucks when you're puking blood. I wasn't a doctor, but I knew that something was majorly wrong with her.

"Yeah. No shit."

I smiled, but it felt strained.

Where the hell was Dastien? I rubbed my sweating palms on my T-shirt.

A minute later, my bedroom door swung open so fast it slammed the wall. I moved to the doorway of the bathroom to see Dastien stride in with Dr. Gonzales behind him. His eyes were glowing a light gold, telling me that his wolf was close to the surface.

Dastien squeezed my hand for a second before squatting next to Meredith. "How are you?"

"How do I look?"

"Pretty terrible."

She did look pretty horrible. Her skin glistened with sweat and was so pale that it looked nearly see-through. Shadows hung under her glass-blue eyes, but it was her slouching shoulders that told me how poorly she felt. Werewolves had the best posture, but she was hunched over like she couldn't even carry the weight of her head.

"Well, at least I look better than I feel," she said.

Dastien grabbed her chin and looked into her eyes. I didn't know what he was doing, but Meredith started to squirm as she tried to avert her gaze. "It's what we thought. Her wolf's awake and fighting her curse."

Dr. Gonzales' stilettos clacked against the tiles as she entered the bathroom. Werewolves might not get sick, but they definitely had a tendency to get into fights. She was around to patch us up.

The doctor always dressed like she was coming from a boardroom meeting. A pale pink blouse with a tie-neck was tucked into her dark gray pencil skirt. Instead of the blazer to finish off the skirt suit, she wore a white lab coat with her name embroidered in blue along the pocket. A black messenger bag held all of her first aid stuff. "We knew this might happen at some point. Can you calm her?" she asked Dastien.

As a strong alpha, Dastien could quiet or rouse the

wolf in any Were. He made a shushing-purring sound at Meredith as he pushed power at her. He'd done it to me before when I felt out of control and it quieted my wolf, but Meredith didn't turn to pudding like I did. Instead, she squirmed, trying to break free from his gaze.

That didn't make any sense. Dastien's shushing always worked.

"She's too far gone. The wolf has been suppressed for so long..." Dastien stepped away, making room for Dr. Gonzales.

"What does that mean?" Meredith said.

"Might be a good idea to sedate her until we figure out other options and inform her parents."

"Why are you talking about me like I'm not here?"

Fear raced through my veins, making me lightheaded. I sat back down on the edge of the tub and Meredith reached for my hand. I twined our fingers together.

This couldn't be happening. Meredith had to be okay.

Dr. Gonzales swung her black messenger bag over her head, and pulled out what looked like a black cosmetics case. I had a feeling it wasn't filled with make-up.

She unzipped the top, and grabbed a shot. For once, I didn't mind seeing her bag full of needles.

"Meredith," she said in a calm, even voice. "I'm going to give you something to make you sleep. When you wake, your wolf should be calm again. Okay?"

Meredith's hand squeezed mine as she nodded.

Dr. Gonzales gripped Meredith's arm and stabbed the needle in. It didn't take long for the drugs to kick in. Dastien caught her as she slid to the floor, lifting her like she weighed nothing. As he put her in bed, I retreated to my room and started pacing.

This shouldn't have happened. I should've pushed her

to talk about her curse and how she was feeling. I knew something was wrong, but I'd let it go.

Stupid. How could I be so stupid?

"Tessa?" Dr. Gonzales' voice brought me back to the present.

"Is she going to be okay?" I asked as I sat down on my bed.

"Can you tell us if something happened with Meredith?"

It didn't go unnoticed that she didn't say that Meredith was going to be okay. She wouldn't lie.

"The curse is still active, but her wolf is awake. Has anything happened to Meredith recently? Anything that could upset her wolf?" the doctor prompted, but I didn't have anything helpful. We went to class, we did homework, and we ate a ton of food. We didn't even get to leave campus very often.

I tried to think of something that could have caused this, but for the life of me, I couldn't. Last night was the first time I'd seen her act off at all. How did she get sick so quickly? "I can't remember anything that really changed. We've been doing our usual stuff since the whole vampire thing."

Dastien came back into the room. I finally really took him in. His navy blue T-shirt was just tight enough to hint at the muscles I knew were underneath. I was glad he'd come so quickly. Having him here made me feel better. Like everything was going to be okay.

"Something's changed," he said. "You know her better than anyone. Did she fight with someone? Get upset? Did someone say something to piss her off? Anything that could bring out her wolf?"

He sat on my bed and gripped my hand. Our bond

strengthened through touch and I could feel his worry on top of my own.

Oh, God. Of course. That was it. "She had a fight with Donovan a few days ago." How could I forget about that?

"What? Why did they fight?" Dr. Gonzales said.

"He left—"

"Right," Dr. Gonzales said. "He had to go find the alphas in South America for the Tribunal. Why would she fight with him about that?"

Mr. Dawson, Donovan, Sebastian, and a few other alphas were off rounding up as many pack leaders as possible for the Tribunal. Some of them lived in pretty remote areas, preferring to be able to switch from wolf to human without worrying who was watching. Donovan had gone after a pack alpha that roamed the Andes Mountains.

I blew out a breath. I didn't know how much to tell them about Donovan and Meredith. It wasn't my business to spill and Meredith liked to keep her stuff private, but she was seriously sick. "When Donovan left last week, he and Meredith had a fight. She wouldn't talk about it, but I have a pretty good guess what they were fighting about."

Dastien leaned closer. "And?"

I paced away from them as I considered what to say. From the sound of Meredith's steady breathing in the next room, she was totally zonked. Screw it. I was gonna spill my guts and hope she wouldn't kick my ass for it later. I turned back to face them. "When they first met, I thought I felt something between Meredith and Donovan. The way they looked at each other was beyond intense. Something clicked with them, but then all the vampire stuff happened... Anyhow, right before Donovan left he told her that he wanted them to be mated, but she refused."

God. She was probably going to kill me for saying this, but if it could save her, then she'd get over it. I reached for Dastien's hand again. "I'm pretty sure they're a true mated pair."

"*Cherie*. Just because we're a mated pair, doesn't mean that others are. It's very rare," Dastien said.

He was going to get himself hit if he kept using that patronizing tone. "I know that I'm new to this whole deal, but I can tell the difference between our bond and other bonds."

Dr. Gonzales stepped closer. "What do you mean?"

I shrugged. "They feel different."

"You can feel bonds?" Dastien asked, spacing his words out so that there was no misunderstanding.

"I guess. Kind of. Can't you feel ours?"

"Sure." There was a hint of a question in the way that he said it.

That didn't sound so convincing. "I don't know why I can tell, but I can. Trust me. They're not like everyone else. Their bond was tangible from the moment they met. The connection between them sizzled, and it got stronger as they spent more time together."

"Assuming you're right, she actually refused him?" Dr. Gonzales' eyebrows were somewhere in the vicinity of her hairline.

Donovan was strong and powerful. It didn't help matters that he was hot and really sweet, too. If I hadn't met Dastien, even I'd be crushing on him. Saying no to him seemed pretty unfathomable. "I think she's being dumb, but Meredith thinks she's 'broken' because of the curse. Like that makes her not worthy of him."

"We need to get Donovan back here," Dr. Gonzales said. "Can you reach him?"

"As soon as he checks in, sure, but that could be today or next week." Dastien rubbed his hands down his face.

"I'm not sure she'll last that long," Dr. Gonzales said.

Panic made my knees weak. I sat on the bed next to Dastien. No. This had to be fixable. We had to fix this. "What do you mean?" I leaned into Dastien as he put his arm around me.

"It typically takes weeks for nausea to set in, but with the blood…Meredith is already considerably past that." She said it gently, as if that would make it any easier to hear. "If we can't find a way to break the curse, she won't have much time."

A loud buzzing rang in my ears.

"Breathe, *cherie*. Take a deep breath."

I did, but it was a shaky one.

We needed a plan.

"Okay," I said when I could speak again. "So, we break the curse or something."

"It's not that easy," Dastien said.

"Nothing ever is." I looked at Dr. Gonzales. "How much time?"

"I'm going to move her to the infirmary and keep her sedated, but her metabolism won't let that work for long."

"That's not answering my question."

Her gaze was full of pity I didn't want. "Two days? Give or take a day."

"Donovan won't make it back before then," Dastien said. "And even if he did get back in time, I don't know how he could fix this. He doesn't have magic to break the curse, and I couldn't get her wolf to listen to me at all. I'm nearly as strong as him."

Holy shit. My chest was tight. There wasn't time to panic, but I was already beyond that. I was nearing a full on freak out.

My heartbeat rang loudly in my ears.

I got up to pace again. There had to be a solution.

The only people who could help were my cousins who belonged to the local coven. Dad took a job at St. Ailbe's so that we could move from LA to Texas, which meant that I could get closer with my *bruja* family. That had never happened. Dastien bit me before we could be reintroduced.

That said, my cousins had helped us before. They'd given me intel and a pretty cool bag of tricks that saved our butts with the vamp situation. I hadn't met anyone else from the coven, but it followed logic that they'd help me again.

This was good. This was a plan. This I could do. "I'm going to call my cousins. Maybe their coven did this to Meredith, but they're my family. It might make a difference if I'm the one asking them to fix it."

"No. That's a crazy idea. Your cousins might have reached out before, but the rest of them... *non*. They're the ones who did this to her in the first place. They let her suffer for years without a second thought."

"I'll convince them that what they did was wrong. I have to."

"I don't want you to take too much of this on yourself," Dr. Gonzales said. "I think you need to start to prepare yourself for what's going to happen." Her words were carefully said and evenly paced, and they made me want to hit her. I didn't like what she was insinuating at all.

"Meredith was there for me when she had no reason to be. She stood by me, and I won't repay her friendship by giving up. I'll find a way fix this."

"Tessa..." Dastien said.

"Don't you start," I said. "I can do this." I wish I really knew that for certain, but I'd do pretty much anything for Meredith. I'd grown up an outcast because of my visions and she'd been the first person that wasn't a member of my immediate family to accept me. She was kind and caring and thoughtful and funny. She deserved to be happy, and she deserved her mate. I was going to help her get that. If I had to beg my cousins for help, I had kneepads. I wouldn't let pride get in the way of saving my best friend.

Dastien got up, brushing a kiss on my forehead. "Call them, and then we'll talk again."

"Okay."

He headed into Meredith's room, lifted her into his arms, and left with Dr. Gonzales.

My alarm went off, telling me it was time to go to the cafeteria before class.

Screw classes. I'd grab some food in the common room downstairs.

I had a curse to break and not much time to do it in.

Chapter Three

In times of crisis, I'd found it best to keep moving forward. I wasn't sure what the right first step was to help Meredith, but I had to do something. Eventually, I'd figure out what would work. I had to.

Calling my brother was at the top of my list. He'd know how to reach the cousins and might have some advice, too. When I first got bitten, he'd hung out with our cousins a few times.

I grabbed my cell and hit Axel's number. He didn't answer. I hung up and called again. No answer.

Shit. He was probably still sleeping off last night's party.

I didn't have my cousins' numbers. This was probably dumb in retrospect, but the two times I'd seen them, I'd been kind of distracted. The first time I'd been in a rush to save Dastien from being eaten by a den of vampires. The second time they'd saved me from getting my ass beat by Imogene.

If anyone would know how to get in touch with them,

Mom would. But she'd ask questions—which was why I'd tried Axel first.

Screw it.

Mom picked up on the first ring.

"Is everything okay?"

I almost laughed. "Why's that the first thing you say when I call?"

"Because lately, every time you call, something's been wrong."

Oh. That kind of blew. And it was totally true. "Right. Well, yes. I'm fine. But no, everything isn't okay."

"What's wrong?"

"Meredith's sick." I hated the sound of that. "I need to talk to Claudia or Raphael. You wouldn't happen to know their numbers or anything, would you?"

"No." Her voice was firm, like I'd just asked her if I could start stripping.

I paced my room. "Mom. Do you—"

"I know where they live, but I don't have their numbers."

Awesome. Maybe this wasn't going as bad as I thought. "Great. Where—"

"I don't think it's a good idea that I tell you, honey. They're all a little…" She sighed. "…*upset* about your situation right now."

I couldn't take that answer. She had to tell me. "I'm not joking. Meredith could die, and I really don't care how upset they are."

"Explain." So, I did. When I got to the end, she was quiet for a minute. "I know you wonder why I didn't bring you back to Texas sooner, but the truth is, I still don't agree with how *La Alquelarre*—the coven—is being run. If you go, they'll try to make you stay. Luciana's in charge, and she isn't a friend of the pack. She'll try to manipulate you, and needing help will make it that much easier."

That sounded like a whole bunch of not fun, but I didn't have a ton of options. "Mom. Please. I'm strong. I'm a werewolf for God's sake and I'm not about to let anyone manipulate me."

"You don't understand. If they have something that you want, they'll…" Mom stopped herself. "I'm worried about what could happen to you."

"You shouldn't worry so much." I had it covered for both of us. "I'm going to be fine, but Meredith might not be." I paused, hoping that would sink in. "The address, please." I squeezed my eyes shut and crossed my fingers.

She was quiet for so long this time, I had to check to make sure she hadn't hung up. "I'm sorry, but I can't. Don't you wonder why I kept you away from them?"

"Sure…" Not that it was relevant right now.

"Your grandmother led the coven because she fulfilled the two requirements: she was female and had the gift of sight. When Luciana took over, your *abuela* started searching for the next generation's leader and found you. We were already in LA because Luciana had everyone fooled. I didn't have any gifts, so she didn't bother pretending around me. *Mija*, she's not a good person, and the coven went dark when she came to power."

I didn't like hearing that this lady had been a total bitch to my mom, but I couldn't let that scare me away. "I get that she's bad, Mom, but that doesn't change the situation that I'm in. I have to go over there. Maybe later I can help straighten out the coven, but not now. I barely have a handle on this werewolf stuff."

"That's not what I meant. It's not your problem anymore. The coven has been in trouble for a long time, and your *abuela* thought it best if we waited to bring you back. After she died, we almost didn't come back at all, but you were having a hard time and your brother was leaving and your powers were growing so strong...so I thought...it doesn't matter. What matters is that going over there now is not a good idea. Not after what's happened. It was dangerous before. It's why we stayed away. But now they feel like the pack wronged them by taking you as their own, and it's even more dangerous. I understand why Dastien did what he did, but he's placed you in a very bad spot. As your mother, I have to protect you. Even when it's hard. Even if it means risking your friend's life. I cannot give you information that could put you at risk."

I wished she had told me this before, but that didn't matter. "But I'm strong, Mom. You have to trust me. I'm a werewolf and a *bruja*. I'll be okay."

"No. I'm sorry, but no."

She couldn't do this. "Mom. Please. I'm begging you. I'll do anything."

"I'll be praying for Meredith. I'll light a *lámpara* for her." She sighed. "*Te quiero mucho, mija.*"

This was not how I wanted this to go. Not at all. Frustration burned in my gut, but there was nothing I could say to Mom that would change her mind. I got my stubbornness from her.

"I love you, too." I barely restrained myself from smashing my phone. Instead, I blew out a breath, and gently placed the phone in my bag. I wasn't giving up that easily.

Dastien knew more than he'd said earlier, and if I couldn't convince him to tell me where my cousins lived, then someone else would.

My stomach growled, which wasn't a good sign. I

needed to eat something before my wolf went totally crazy.

I made my way to the common room. The fridge was well-stocked with all kinds of snacks, prepared meals, and treats. I grabbed five sandwiches, a jumbo bag of chips, an orange Fanta, and shoved everything in my bag. Not the best breakfast ever, but it'd do.

I left the dorms and went in search of Dastien.

***

My mate proved harder to find than I'd thought. He wasn't in any of his usual haunts—the cafeteria, the gym, or on the Cazadores course, the totally nuts obstacle course used to train super badass werewolf warriors. I was two-and-a-half sandwiches in before I finally found him in Mr. Dawson's office.

While Mr. Dawson was away tracking down pack alphas for the Tribunal, Dastien was in charge of St. Ailbe's. I was proud that Dastien was strong enough to control all the werewolves in the school, but having him in charge was awkward since I was still a senior. Though no one seemed to care about that besides me.

Mr. Dawson's secretary was at her desk, typing away outside his door. Mrs. Kilburn's gray hair was pulled back in a tidy bun at the nape of her neck and her olive green cardigan was buttoned to her neck. It seemed a little much for summer, but who was I to judge? I used to wear gloves year round.

She waved me past without looking up from her computer. I knocked once and opened the door.

Dastien was seated behind Mr. Dawson's massive desk. "You didn't go to class?"

I raised an eyebrow at that. Did he actually think I was

going to go study Shakespeare while this was going on? "No. I didn't go to class."

"Right." He drew out the word a bit, but didn't ask why. He knew why.

I sat in one of the big brown leather chairs, and Dastien came around to sit on the desk in front of me.

"Any word on Donovan?" Please, let him say yes. Please, for the love of all that is good, let him say yes.

"No."

Crap.

"But I don't expect to for at least another day or two." He sighed. "I wish you would've told me what was going on with them. I thought we weren't keeping things from each other."

"I wasn't keeping something from you. It was their private business and I figured when Donovan got back, we could play matchmakers. Force a double-date or something." I slouched back in the chair and closed my eyes. "Now I just want to keep her alive. I can't lose her."

Dastien trailed his fingers down my cheek and I opened my eyes. He was sitting on his heels in front of my chair. "We'll find a way to fix this." He pointed at my purse. "You're going somewhere?"

"Yes?" I gave him my best angelic smile. "I'm going to see my cousins. You know where they are, right?"

"Yes." He pressed his lips in a fine line. "But no. I'm not telling you."

This was getting old. "I'm really tired of hearing 'no' today."

"If that's what you want to talk about, then that's all I've got for you."

I didn't want to fight with him, but this wasn't okay. "You don't get to make decisions for me."

"No. You will *not* be going to see any member of that coven." He backed his command with power.

I let his words slip past me. Anger heated my skin. "Did you just order me not to do something?"

He had the intelligence to look ashamed. "I'm sorry." He stood up. "But I can't let you go there. It's not safe."

"My mom said the same thing." I reached for his hand, and twined his fingers with mine. "But I'm not listening to either of you. I think you both are forgetting that Meredith's life is at stake. They could help."

"I'd feel better about you going if you'd shifted. If you did it right now, it wouldn't take long, and you'd still have plenty of time to—"

Was he trying to bribe me into shifting? "No. I know I've been pushing it off and I'm running out of time with the Tribunal and all, but Meredith needs my help *now*." I didn't want to fight with him about this, but I had to go with or without his approval.

"You don't understand…"

"Then explain it to me."

He crossed his arms, and leaned against the desk. "There was a time when we were on good terms, friendly even, with the local coven. I grew up here with Michael and used to play with your cousins and the rest of the younger coven members."

I knew that he saw Mr. Dawson as a friend and sort of father figure, but it always weirded me out how he called Mr. Dawson by his first name. I had no idea he knew any of *La Aquelarre*.

"That all stopped when your grandmother died. Luciana has a thing against the wolves…I know some people, like Meredith, kept in contact with the coven, but most of them hate us. Really, truly hate us. Luciana's instilled that in them, and that's only escalated since I bit you."

He was totally backing up what Mom said, but that didn't change what I needed to do. No matter how bad or dangerous this Luciana was, I had to ask the coven for help. Why didn't they get that Meredith's life was worth the risk?

I cracked my knuckles as I took in what he'd said. "So, they're holding a grudge?"

"That's putting it mildly. I bit their next leader. What I did…it would've been big deal even if we were on good terms. They're not okay with what happened. And they won't be for a while, if ever." He ran his thumb back and forth over the back of my hand. "I wasn't going to tell you, but they've also asked to speak at the Tribunal."

Oh, no. "That sounds a whole lot of *no bueno.*"

He shrugged, making it seem like it wasn't that big of a deal, but I knew better. "It's not like the Tribunal was ever going to be fun. I think we—I—have a strong case, but they're not helping. They're talking about fighting us. Taking you back. It's not a good situation."

"God. Talk about burying the lead. You say I held back with that stuff about Meredith and Donovan, but how could you not tell me about this?"

"I didn't want to worry you."

"That's not really an option. If something's up, you have to tell me."

"I'm sorry. I probably should've said something sooner, but that doesn't change my opinion. No matter how badly you might want it, curing Meredith might not be something you can do."

I refused to believe that. "Doing something is better than doing nothing."

He squeezed my hand. "I'm hoping Donovan gets back to us soon. He might know some way to help her that we haven't thought of yet. It's a long shot, but... And if they're true mates, then he might sense that something's wrong with her, too. Her parents will be here tomorrow, and her brothers are on their way, too." Meredith had four older brothers, all of them Cazadores. I'd seen pictures. They looked like Norse gods—tall, blond, and blue-eyed.

I was glad they were all coming, but there wasn't any reason to believe they'd be able to do anything except watch Meredith die.

"The best thing you can do right now is go to class."

No. The best thing I could do right then was to find a way to break the spell. I couldn't go to class, but he didn't have to know. "Sure." I hated lying to him. It was just plain wrong, but he wasn't giving me any choice.

"Hey," he said with a small smile.

"What?"

"You know I love you, right?"

I almost rolled my eyes. "Yeah." He was being sweet after telling me no, but it was sucking me in all the same.

"I'm proud of you and how far you've come. I couldn't have picked a better mate."

Why did he have to be nice right after I lied to him? It was making me feel all kinds of horrible. "Thanks. I'm trying."

"Not trying. Doing. So proud of you." He pressed his lips against mine. I ran my hands through his hair and the world faded away as I melted into the kiss. He had this ability to wipe away all thoughts. All I wanted was more. Of him. I moaned and his hands squeezed my hips as he pulled me closer. When we finally moved apart, we were both out of breath.

He pressed his forehead to mine. "Bye, *cherie*."

My legs were a little unsteady as I walked away. I looked over my shoulder at him before I walked out the door. He was reclining against the front of the desk, with his ankles crossed and his hands shoved in his pockets. He winked, and I got that butterflies-in-the-belly feeling.

He was going to be so pissed when he found out what I was doing.

I made my way to the next building. The courtyard was empty and the sounds of the outdoors that surrounded the school filled my short walk—grass crunching under my feet, birds chirping, and small animals foraging for food. The dorm buildings and cafeterias were to my right. On my left, buildings that housed the classrooms cast shadows over the quad.

I stepped into the academic building and took the stairs two at a time. The hallway was empty, only the faint murmuring of the classes in session could be heard. Lockers lined the walls, each with a nameplate instead of a number, and not a single one with a lock.

After Meredith, Chris was my closest friend at school. He'd literally caught me the first time I tried to escape campus, and his humor had gotten me through the first week. The only downside was that he initially had a little bit of a thing for me, but we'd gotten past that. Thankfully.

Chris was overly friendly with everyone, and he was my next best resource for finding my cousins. He had normal, human physics second period. Not to be confused with the totally wacky metaphysics—a class designed to try to scientifically explain the supernatural.

I peeked in the tiny, off-center window of his classroom door and spotted his head of wavy blond hair in the back of the room. A teacher I hadn't met yet gestured wildly with a piece of chalk, then slammed his hand on the black board next to his scribblings for emphasis. The back of his black hair was standing on end, giving him an Einstein-esque look. If Einstein were ripped and thirty.

He motioned wildly again and the class cracked up. Holy crap. The guy was either a really great teacher or completely insane.

I knocked a couple of times before opening the door wide enough to stick my head in. "Sorry to interrupt, but I need Christopher Matthews, please."

A couple of the guys started whistling, and I couldn't stop the burn from spreading across my cheeks. The maturity level in this classroom was shockingly low.

The teacher crossed his arms, unintentionally rubbing chalk over his shirt. Perfect. He was pissed, which I totally understood. I'd ruined his flow.

"We're in the middle of class."

"I know, but I need Chris now." And I didn't have time for this.

"Whatever you need him for can wait until after class."

I could feel my eyes changing. The hair on my arms stood on end, and I forced myself to relax.

I will not grow fur. I will not grow fur.

The third time I repeated it in my head, I was calmer.

"I'm afraid it can't wait. Chris is leaving class now. I'm not asking." I met the teacher's gaze as I spoke. I didn't know him, but I knew that I was alpha enough to turn my request into a demand. One he'd have to obey. We held gazes for a second before he turned to Chris.

Fantastic. Some people might like displays of power, but I totally didn't. Not at all. They kind of made me feel ill. The classroom had grown completely silent as they waited to see if I'd do something more.

I cleared my throat and glanced at Chris—the only person who was still looking at me. "I'll wait for you by your locker."

Chris rolled his shoulders back, calling to attention his toned arms. He might prefer to draw, but he could kick his fair share of ass, too. He stuck his pencil behind his ear and quickly gathered his things. Satisfied that he was coming, I gave the teacher one last look and left.

As Chris strode to me, blond hair falling into his eyes, I swung his locker open.

"What's going on?" He said as he shoved in his books.

"I'll tell you once we get outside." I didn't want anyone listening. The walls of St. Ailbe's were thick, but werewolves had impossibly good hearing. I couldn't risk anyone stopping us.

As soon as we were through the door, he pulled me to a stop. "What's going on?" He asked again.

"It's Meredith. Her wolf woke, and the curse...it's going to kill her. She was puking blood this morning."

His blue eyes widened. "Shit."

"I know."

He rested his hands on his head as he said some choice expletives. I tried to keep my emotions in control as he let his go. Meredith had been his friend for way longer than I had. I'd already had my freak out time, so I let him have his.

He paced in a circle a few times before stopping in front of me. "What do we do?"

"We ask my cousins for help. If they can't break the curse and I can't convince whoever cast it to break it, then I'm not sure what'll be next, but we'll cross that bridge later. Or hopefully not at all." I crossed my fingers. "You wouldn't happen to know where the coven is, would you?"

"No."

Shit.

"No one except Mr. Dawson—and maybe Dastien—knows were they live. Did you ask Dastien?"

I cringed. "That's a no go."

"I can get us in the general area, but it won't be exactly where they live."

I grabbed my car keys out of my purse. That I could work with. "Get us close, and I'll use my visions to find the rest of the way there."

Chris swallowed. "Can I see her before we go?"

I wanted to say yes, but we didn't have time and I didn't want us to get caught. "She's in the infirmary, but she's knocked out. She'll be there when we get back."

"Okay. Let's go," he said.

My fast walk quickly turned into a jog.

God, I hoped we had enough time.

Chapter Four

Chris directed me down the most pothole-ridden road I'd ever seen. My Tiguan SUV bottomed-out and I cringed. This puppy was only weeks old, but I had to push her hard, driving as fast as I could.

We came around a bend, and I slowed as an unmarked fork appeared ahead. "Which way?"

"I don't know," Chris said. "Maybe right? Probably right."

"Maybe or probably?"

"I don't know. I've never been this close. Wolves aren't usually allowed on their land, but I'm pretty sure it's up here somewhere."

I pulled over, and tapped my fingers on the steering wheel. "No worries. I'll figure this out." I undid my seatbelt and hopped down from the car.

"Where are you going?" Chris asked, leaning halfway out his door.

"Just wait." I closed my eyes and let down my mental barriers. Visions used to bombard me all the time, but now I had to lower the imaginary wall around my mind to see anything. I pressed my hands against the dirt road, hoping for something, but all I got were flashes of cars driving by. I walked a little farther down. A rabbit met its maker here. Not helpful. I touched the trees and a bush, and got a whole bunch of nothing useful.

The irony wasn't lost on me. I'd spent my whole life wishing for the visions to go away, but now, when I actually needed one, they were failing me.

I went down one of the forks in the road, bending to touch the ground, searching for any sign that I was headed in the right direction.

After a bit, I turned around and started down the other fork.

"You see anything?" Chris asked from beside the car.

"Nothing useful, but I'm not giving up yet." Touching the trees showed me the days passing. Sunlight. Rain. Animals climbing up their bark.

I saw visions of cars going both directions, but there was no way to tell which fork was the way to *La Aquelarre.*

"Screw it." I yelled back at Chris. "Let's pick one. There's a fifty-fifty chance we'll get lucky. And if we don't, then we turn around and try the other way."

"Sounds like a plan," Chris said.

On my walk back to the car I spotted a clue. It was barely visible, but the speck of white hit the sun just enough to catch my eye.

I stepped to the other side of the street, and kicked away the dirt.

A Whataburger cup. I tried not to get my hopes up as I wiped my hands on my jeans. I said a prayer and grabbed it.

"Don't mess with that shit, dude," said a guy with *spiky blond hair and a thick Texas accent. He swirled the*

straw in his milkshake before taking a big drink. "You don't want to fuck with the wolves. You're gonna get us all in trouble."

Music played in the car. I recognized the distinctive style of Calle 13's reggaeton. Fast food wrappers were piled on the floorboard of the backseat.

"We used to hang out with them." The guy driving had black hair and dark brown eyes. "Dastien was always cool to me. Intruding during their proceedings is messed up. My mom's gonna get us into trouble."

Holy shit. They were talking about Dastien and the Tribunal. It was good to know not all of them were against us.

"All I'm saying is that your mother has an extreme hatred for wolves. Going against her is a huge risk, especially now that Teresa's turned and we have no back-up leader."

They took the fork on the right.

The guy with the shake swirled the cup around before taking a long slurp.

The other guy snorted. "Mom's lost her mind. I don't trust whatever she's seeing in those visions of hers. I think she started this whole thing to begin with." His fingers tapped the steering wheel to the beat of the music. "They've been nothing but nice to us. Yeah, what happened to Teresa sucked, but it can't be undone. Going to war isn't going to solve anything. What we need is a replacement. It's dumb as all hell not to have a back-up..."

Ugh. I hated being called Teresa. But I agreed with the guy. Why didn't they have a back-up? I didn't like feeling responsible for them being left without a leader. For the first time, I felt bad about having been bitten for a reason that wasn't focused on my problems.

The blond guy took another sip of his shake. The loud slurping signaled that he'd finished. "Just be careful with that shit. She might be your mother, but she's not right in the head. We don't have anyone who can stand against her. Not anymore." He threw the cup out of the window.

Even her own son thought she was dangerous. This was definitely not a good sign.

"Get in the car," I said as I ran back. "You were right about the fork."

He laughed. "See, babe. You should never question my genius."

I snorted. "Some ego you got there, Mr. Matthews."

As soon as we were buckled in, I floored it down the road. We took a sharp corner too quickly and I had to swerve so I didn't run off the road. "Crap. Sorry."

Chris had his hand on the 'oh shit' bar. "Maybe you should slow it down, Speedy Gonzales?"

"I should but we're in a hurry." A metal farm gate blocked the road, and I slammed the brakes. "Can you get that for me?"

"I have a bad feeling about this. You sure we're in the right place?"

"As sure as I can be when I have no idea where the hell I'm going. There haven't been any more forks and we're out of road. Unless the guys from my vision were heading somewhere else, this should be it."

Chris grunted and hopped down from the car. The gate squeaked as he opened it. It seemed silly for it to be there and not have a lock. Who was it really keeping out?

I eased through the gate. The tires rattled over the spaced out metal rails of the cattle guard that lined the entrance. Goosebumps rose along my skin as an icky sensation slipped off me. It was as if bad juju was warning me away from going through it.

When Chris got back in the car, his eyes were glowing blue—a sign that his wolf was close to the surface—but he didn't say a word.

Something felt off. It was too quiet in my head. I took inventory, trying to figure out what was wrong.

Oh my God. I couldn't feel Dastien anymore.

"Can you feel the pack?" I asked Chris.

"No. My pack bond dulled when we got on their land. It's making me edgy."

"Weird."

"Very."

I brushed it off, and focused on what we were there to do. We needed to get in, find my cousins, and leave before we could get into any trouble.

No big deal.

My Tiguan rounded another corner and the road smoothed out. The dense treeline thinned to reveal little two-story cottages lining the dirt road. Cars and SUVs were parked haphazardly on the roadside. If the cars hadn't been there, it would've looked like an Old West town.

"It's kind of creepy that they have a mini-suburb out here, right?" I asked.

"Supernaturals like to stick together. It makes life easier when you don't have to constantly pretend to be normal."

That made sense. I was terrible at the whole pretending stuff with the visions. Being a pariah among norms was all too familiar.

"I'm not gonna lie, my wolf isn't liking it. I'm getting itchy." Chris' eyes were still glowing. That didn't bode well for us either.

I handed him a pair of sunglasses that Dastien had

stashed in my car. "Dude. If you can't calm it down, how am I going to stay in control?"

"I don't know." He slid them on. "I think we should turn around."

Yeah, that wasn't an option. I stopped the car in the middle of the road. "You can wait for me outside the gate if you want."

"No. I can't. Dastien would kill me if I left you alone to face the witches. I'm surprised he let you come at all."

I bit my lip. "Well…"

"You've got to be fucking kidding me." Chris slammed his hand on the dash. "He didn't let you come?"

I resented that. "No one bosses me around. We're here to help Meredith. And I shouldn't need his permission anyhow."

Someone knocked on my window and I jumped.

Smooth move, Tessa. I should've been paying better attention.

The guy from my vision—Luciana's son—motioned for me to roll down my window. "And you are?" He asked.

"I'm here to see Claudia and Raphael," I said. "I'm their cousin."

"Teresa?" He wasn't giving anything away with his stoic face.

When I nodded, he stepped back. "Park there." He pointed to the side of the road.

I did so quickly, then grabbed my bag and hopped down.

The guy was waiting for me in the center of the road. "I'm Daniel," he said. His face was too empty—a perfect emotionless mask. I'd gotten used to everyone towering over my five feet and change, but Daniel was only a few inches taller than me. Even if he was a bit on the short side, he stood the way someone does when they have a lot of power. Tall, shoulders back, head held high. He looked me in the eye, and I had to fight the urge to enter into a staring contest.

My wolf started to rise. She didn't want anyone challenging her. The itch to change and lash out at him rose in me. I fought it down, but pain ran through my limbs.

I couldn't let this happen.

Chris growled as he stepped in front of me, cutting off Daniel's line of sight.

Daniel grinned as he peered around Chris. His mask slid away, making him seem a little more approachable. "It's good to finally meet you, although I wish it'd been before…"

Right. Before I'd been bitten.

He held out his hand, and I hesitated. If I was being honest with myself, I wanted to see something from him. Especially after my earlier vision. But it was an invasion of privacy.

My mental debate didn't last long. Turned out, I wanted information more than I cared about Daniel's privacy.

I took his hand, letting myself open to my *bruja* side. It took a fraction of a second for me to relax just a little more, and—

"The wolves have taken her for their own," said a woman. She was about my mother's age and wore a skirt that skimmed the floor. Her frizzy brown hair was braided and pinned on top of her head in a halo. "You have to bring her back."

Great. She was talking about me.

"And how am I supposed to do that, Mom?" Daniel

43

asked. "What's done is done."

"No. We can get rid of her wolf."

Daniel was pissed. And sad. I'd made him sad when I turned. That wasn't something I ever expected.

"You do that and the wolves will come for us. You're starting—"

"They started it by taking our next leader. She's a strong bruja. And now she's one of them—"

Daniel pulled away, and I was back in the present.

This confirmed what Dastien and my mother said, but I wasn't sure that I could fix the coven. Or if I even wanted to. It wasn't like I could be a pack alpha and rule a coven, too. Honestly, I wasn't sure I wanted either.

I cleared my throat, trying to buy myself time to shake the vision. "Sorry."

"That's okay," Daniel said. "What did you see?"

"Nothing much." I lied.

"It's been a while, Chris," Daniel said, acknowledging Chris for the first time.

"Three years." Chris had a natural dry rasp in his voice, but his tone of voice was a little rougher than usual. He wouldn't be able to take those glasses off anytime soon.

Daniel stared him in the eyes. It didn't matter that there was a pair of sunglasses blocking the gaze from Chris. From the way Chris was standing, completely rigid, every muscle tense, I knew we were seconds away from a code red.

Daniel started to smell like campfire with a hint of sulfur. I'd come to recognize the scent as extreme anger. I took that as my cue to intervene. "My cousin's house would be?"

"Fourth on the right." He motioned with a nod.

I started down the road, dragging Chris beside me.

"Teresa," Daniel said.

I ground my teeth. I loathed it when people called me that. Not even my parents used my full name, except when they were extremely pissed. "Yeah?" I glanced at him.

"It would be good if you came back sometime."

If I hadn't seen those visions, I wouldn't have noticed the plea behind his words. My wolf settled down. He wasn't a threat. Not right now. But coming back? That wasn't happening. It was enough of a risk to come when Meredith was so sick. I wasn't about to pop over for social calls. "Probably not a good idea. I'm not totally under control."

"We can help with that."

Chris growled.

Yeah, that had worked out real well for Meredith... The bad thing was that if he'd asked me when I first woke up as a werewolf, I might have taken him up on it. But not anymore. "Not interested. Thanks for the offer, though."

His shoulders slumped for a fraction of a second before he stood tall again and nodded. "The door is open if you ever change your mind."

"Sure. Thanks." But I was never going to take him up on it in this lifetime.

"They want you back?" Chris asked so softly, I could barely hear the words.

"They're all mad that I'm a wolf," I said back, my voice equally soft. "They want me here so badly that they're planning on speaking against Dastien at the Tribunal."

"Shit."

"Yep." Even if I was supposed to be their leader, I couldn't imagine why they'd be so desperate to have me join. There had to be someone else in my generation with the gift of sight that could take it over. If I could find someone, then maybe they'd drop this whole vendetta against the pack.

Unless there was a bigger agenda. I thought back to the vision and the mention of a war.

Christ. There was no way I had time to worry about that right then. I shoved it to the back of my mind for another day.

In the short time it took to get to the fourth house, people of all ages—some in hippy gear, some in normal clothes—started to congregate on porches. Daniel stood in the middle of the road talking to a few others. They were all eyeballing us. Most stared at Chris like he was the enemy. Some looked at me like I was, too. Most seemed simply curious. Their eyes lingered on me a little longer.

Good thing I was used to being stared at. You didn't get through seventeen years of visions by letting weird looks bother you.

I shoved everything out of my mind except finding answers about Meredith. I was here for a purpose, and losing sight of that wouldn't be good for anyone.

The wooden stairs to my cousins' doorstep creaked as I walked up.

"Let's get in and out," Chris said.

"My thoughts exactly." I knocked once and before I could knock a second time, Claudia answered.

Her thick, pin-straight, black hair was split into two braids. She wore a pair of jean cut-offs and a T-shirt. "*Prima.* What're you doing here?" Her eyes were wide.

"I need your help."

She looked beyond Chris and me, taking in all the people gathered around. She pressed her lips together. "Let's go inside," she said after a second.

"Thanks. I think that's best."

Every inch of the living room was filled with tchotchkes. The place was a dust mite's haven, but not a speck of dust tainted the decor. The walls were lined with shelves filled to the brim with figurines, and covered with cutesy plaques with proverbs and sayings. Little dishes of potpourri sat on almost every flat surface. The scent of rose, cinnamon, orange, clove, and at least a dozen other things filled the air. The effect was only slightly nauseating.

The back wall held an altar with lit candles in skinny, tall glass jars with images of the saints on them. A framed portrait of Our Lady of Guadalupe hung above the candles.

Claudia motioned us to the cushy floral printed couch. "Can I get you something to drink?"

I sat down. "No. I'm fine."

Chris shook his head and sat next to me. He took his sunglasses off, hanging them off the neck of his T-shirt. His eyes were finally back to their normal, non-glowing blue. I was glad his wolf was wrapped up, because mine wasn't. Daniel's comments plus missing the connection to Dastien was making my wolf uneasy. Not enough to make me shift, but it was more than enough to put me on edge.

Claudia settled on a blue velvet chair. She tugged on one of her braids before flipping it over her shoulder. "I'm glad you came. It's been tense here."

"I'm getting that. Loudly. I spoke with Daniel for a minute... I hope you all know that I'm not leaving my pack. I'm happy where I am." Chris started to move, but I put my hand on his knee, stilling him.

"I get it, and for the record—we're divided on that. The majority of us want you to stay where you are."

I was too relieved to be insulted that they didn't want me around. "Good. I'd rather not have this problem become bigger than it should be. Is there anything I can do to help sway the rest?"

"No, but I'll let you know if I think of something." She smiled, but it didn't reach her eyes. "Not to be rude, but why are you here?"

I was more than happy to focus in on my real goal. "You know my friend, Meredith?"

"Of course. A few of the coven members liked to hang out with the wolves a while back. Even though we're not exactly friendly now, we still keep tabs on the pack members."

I don't know why it surprised me, but it did. And whatever 'tabs' *La Aquelarre* had on us, they must've been pretty damned accurate. The day I'd met my cousins, they'd shown up with backpacks filled with weapons made specifically for Meredith and me. "She started throwing up blood this morning."

Claudia paled, giving away that she knew exactly what that meant.

"She doesn't have long. Maybe a day or two." I leaned toward her. "If there's anything you can do, I'd be grateful."

Raphael came through the back door. His khaki shorts were fraying along the bottom hems.

Claudia nodded at him before answering me. "The only way to help would be to get Luciana to break her spell, but there's no way she'd do that."

"Why not? I can be pretty convincing."

Claudia made a face. "She's happy to have one less wolf to worry about."

What the hell? She would let an innocent teenager die because she didn't like werewolves? What was her problem with our kind?

"And messing with someone else's spell is trouble," Raphael continued where Claudia left off. "The chances of you actually breaking it...let's just say they're not great."

Chris sat straighter. "What do you mean? I thought it was only a matter of finding the right spell to counter it."

Raphael chuckled.

"Not with this spell," Claudia said. "Imagine it's like a twisted web of sticky bubble gum. If you put your hands in to untangle the mess, you'll get it more tangled at best. Most likely, some of the spell will stick to you."

Fantastic. "So, how do you break one?"

Raphael crossed his arms, and stared down at me. It wasn't an unfriendly stare—there wasn't any anger in it— but an assessing one. "The best way is to get the person who cast it to break it. It's their will that binds it. They let that go, and the spell is gone."

This wasn't what I wanted to hear. At all. "There has to be another way. From what I've heard, Luciana isn't going to break this spell. I can't go back without a plan."

Claudia and her twin brother shared a long look.

He shook his head. "Don't do it," he said, finally.

"They were supposed to be hers anyhow. Does it really matter now that the situation's changed a bit?" she said.

"Luciana'll be pissed if she finds out."

I wasn't sure what they were arguing about, but I wasn't about to question them. I needed all the help I could get.

She shrugged. "She's always pissed. At least now she'll have a reason." Claudia left the room.

Chris was silent beside me. I wondered what he thought of all of this, but knowing him, I'd probably get an earful when we got back in the car.

Claudia came back with a small stack of books. "Take

them. They might help you think outside the box."

Two of the three books were old, their pages yellowed and the corners of their covers bent and worn. They smelled of leather and dust and vanilla. The third booked looked brand new.

These weren't an answer to my problem exactly, but maybe they could lead to one. I put them in my messenger bag. "Thank you."

Claudia gave me a small shrug. "You should've gotten them years ago." She paused. "But it'd be best if you didn't show them to anyone. They're meant to be seen by coven members only."

That part was going to be difficult. I might be a *bruja*, but besides my visions, I didn't know the first thing about magic. I'd definitely need some help deciphering everything. "I can promise that only people I absolutely trust will know about these."

Claudia was taking another risk for me, and I appreciated it. She'd helped bring me the info and tools to find the vampire caves and fight them, saved my ass from getting creamed by Imogene, and now, she and Raphael were helping me again. "If you ever need anything from me, if there is anything I can ever help you with, let me know."

"Thanks. I'll take you up on it."

I nudged Chris. "Let's go."

When Chris and I stepped outside, a crowd of at least twenty was waiting. "You don't think they're here to tar and feather us, do you?" I asked Chris softly.

"I'd love for them to try. I haven't gotten my workout in today." He slipped the sunglasses back on, covering his glowing eyes.

Perfect. This was a disaster waiting to happen.

The people parted and the lady from my vision stepped up to the house. She was wearing the same outfit as I'd seen her in earlier. Long flowing skirt. Frizzy hair braided and pinned in a halo on the crown of her head.

She smiled softly at us, but her eyes were too harsh to ever be mistaken as kind. "Hello, Teresa."

"Hi, Luciana." What was with the *brujos* and my given name?

Chris stood behind me with a hand on my shoulder. He was ready to step in if needed.

"I hoped you'd come before now," she said.

"I came because your spell has made Meredith Molloney extremely sick."

"And you think I should break it?"

Even if it was a long shot, I had to at least try. "Yes. If there were some way to convince you…"

She grinned, but it made me shiver. "I think we could come to an arrangement."

I was pretty sure I didn't like where this was going, but there was no guarantee the books would help Meredith. I walked down a step. "What kind of arrangement are we talking about?"

"Nothing too big." Her smile widened, and it made me more nervous. Like a monster was getting ready to swallow me whole. "I'd like for you to live here, where you belong. To study with us and learn our ways."

The people watching were completely still and silent, waiting for my response.

It'd come in handy to know more *bruja* stuff. I actively wanted to know more about it and learn more about my abilities, but there was no way I was leaving St. Ailbe's. The place had grown on me, and I liked being close to Dastien and far away from Luciana. "What about the pack?"

She spread her hands wide. "You'd be training to take over the coven when I'm ready to step down, like we'd always planned. You'd have to leave the pack."

That's what I thought she meant, and it so wasn't happening. "Even if I wanted to leave the pack, which I don't...at all...what makes you think I have any aspirations to lead the coven?"

"Everyone wants power." A few members of the coven nodded their heads.

I snorted. "Not me. And you're forgetting one tiny, little thing. I'm a *werewolf.*"

Shit. The look she gave me told me I'd stepped into her trap. Chris must've known it too because his hand tightened on my shoulder.

"I could take care of that if I cast the same spell on you that I cast on Meredith."

I swallowed down a growl, barely. The people closest to me took a step back. Except Luciana. She took a step forward.

"Your wolf would go into hibernation," Luciana kept talking, ignoring my reaction. "You wouldn't feel any pain. Your emotions would be under control again, and you wouldn't have to fear shifting ever again."

I had to hand it to her. She knew exactly what buttons to push. Yes, my emotions being all wonky bugged the crap out of me. I didn't enjoy feeling out of control. And yeah, I was still a little freaked out about the whole shifting thing, but that didn't mean I wanted to end it all. I was adjusting. Slower than Dastien—and pretty much everyone else—would like, but I was adjusting all the same.

"This lady is a freaking nut job. We should go. Now,"

Chris whispered in his barely-audible way.

I grunted quietly. Luciana wouldn't get to me. I wouldn't give her the satisfaction. I fisted my hands by my sides. "News flash, lady. Your spell doesn't work. Meredith's dying. She's literally wasting away as we speak. Even if I hated being a Were, why would I risk it?"

"There wouldn't be a risk. Meredith was born with her wolf, you weren't. It'll be easy to cut it off. And if it did wake, I'd be there to put her down."

Put her down. My nails lengthened, drawing blood as I kept my hands tightly fisted.

The crowd took another step back, but two people stepped forward. Daniel and a girl. Back-up. But for who? Me or Luciana?

This was going to turn into a situation if I didn't get a grip on my wolf, but she wanted to rip Luciana's throat out.

Chris pushed some power toward me, trying to keep me calm. It wasn't as potent as Dastien's, but it was enough. That said, Chris was right. We needed to leave before anything bad happened. "Thanks for the offer, but no." My words were sharp. "I don't want anyone else messing with who I am."

"I wouldn't be messing with who you are. I'd just be putting you back the way you were before you were attacked by rabid dogs. We can overlook your mutt connection, but only if you—"

"Excuse me? Did you just call me a *mutt*?" My voice was gravelly and lower than usual.

Luciana muttered something, and it felt like something slapped my face.

Red filled my vision. I tried to lunge, but Chris held me back. I spun, snarling at him. Before I could order him to

53

let me go, he clapped his hand over my mouth. He looped his other arm around my waist, holding me firmly against him as my bones popped. "We're leaving," he said.

Fur spread along my arms, and I growled. The need to take Luciana down was stronger than anything I'd ever felt before. It was like fire in my veins.

Chris dragged me to the car and shoved me in the driver's side. He kept pushing me until I was on the passenger's side. I went for the door.

I couldn't leave without putting Luciana in her place. I wanted blood.

Chris hit the locks before I could open the door and put the car in gear.

I raged and yelled, growling nonsense as I tried to get the car door open.

"Stop," Chris commanded as he pulled a u-turn on someone's lawn, speeding toward the open gate.

When we hit the cattle guard, I felt that slick feeling again, like we were passing through a barrier. But this time it didn't just feel slimy. Now, it burned my skin like sandpaper against a bad sunburn. It was painful enough to shock my wolf. My bones cracked back in place and fur slid away.

"Holy fuck," I said, gasping. "Do you feel that?"

His gaze stayed on the road. "I felt something alright."

I rubbed my arms, trying to ease the sensation, but the pain lingered. "Let's get the hell out of here."

"No problem." He floored it down the bumpy dirt road.

Something was wrong. Did I forget something back there?

The further we got from the coven's land, the more my fear grew. My heart was pumping so fast, so loud, it was echoing in my ears.

This wasn't right. I was safe. My wolf had nearly gotten me into big trouble, but Chris had gotten us away in time. My fear shouldn't be getting worse.

"Are you okay?" Chris said.

"I don't know." I swallowed. "I'm so afraid, but I have no idea why. We got away from there. I'm fine. You're fine. Why am I freaking out?"

And then it hit me. "Go faster. Drive." I spotted him in the distance. A wolf running down the side of the road. "Stop. Stop the car. Now. Please." I slapped Chris on the arm. "Now!"

"Okay. Okay." He slammed on the brakes, and my seatbelt strained to keep me in my seat. "Is that who I think that is?"

"Yes." For once, it wasn't my own fear I was feeling. It was Dastien's. I couldn't imagine what would make him so afraid, but whatever it was, I wanted it gone.

I un-clicked my seatbelt, jumped down from the car, and started running to meet him.

1

Chapter Five

Dastien bounded toward me in wolf-form. I stopped in the middle of the dirt road and he tackled me to the ground. Thank God we'd done so much training lately. I knew how to take a fall without hurting anything. Or, more accurately, without hurting anything too badly. I hit the road, careful to curl into my stomach so my head wouldn't slam into the compacted dirt. Wolf-Dastien ran his nose over every inch of me. He growled when he got to my hand and then licked it. And then sneezed on it.

"Gross." I wiped my hand off.

He did the wolf-version of a grunt, which came out more like a whine.

When he was done with his inspection, he plopped down on top of me and rubbed his nose against my neck.

"Jeez. You weigh a million pounds. Get off." I tried to move him but he wouldn't budge. "Babe. I can't breathe."

He got up and pushed his forehead to mine. His relief was staggering, but the terror that something had happened to me still bubbled under the surface. He growled, and his alpha-ness ran through me. My skin stretched and itched.

He was bringing out my wolf. My heart raced. "Stop." My insides mushed around as I tried to fight the change. "Cut it out." I met his gaze. "Stop it right now!" I threw as much power as I could into the command and he instantly calmed down and stepped back.

I sat up, breathing like I'd run miles. "What the hell's wrong with you?"

He howled.

Great. I didn't speak wolf. "Chris? What's his problem?" The fear and anxiety that Dastien was still giving off made me on edge, ready to attack some unknown enemy.

"Honestly, I have no idea," he said from the driver's seat.

I stood up and brushed the dirt off my jeans. My bum was a little sore from the fall. "Maybe next time don't tackle me so hard, okay?"

"I could give him a few lessons on tackling—"

Dastien growled, cutting off Chris. When I'd first gotten to St. Ailbe's and tried to make a run for it, Chris had chased me through campus and tackled me mid-shift. Then, he'd hit on me while I was trapped beneath him and he was still naked from shifting, which my mate now took exception to.

Dastien brushed against my hip—not giving me even an inch of room as I went to the trunk. When it wouldn't open, I banged on the hatch. "Unlock it, please," I said to Chris.

The lock clicked and I grabbed a pair of sweats and flip-flops for Dastien. Meredith had stashed some stuff in the trunk after the whole vampire thing. Apparently, all Weres should have at least a few pairs of sweats and flip-flops in their cars for emergencies. I dropped pants, a T-shirt, and the sandals on the ground by Dastien, and zipped up the bag.

By the time I closed the hatch, Dastien was back in his two-legged form. He was wearing the pants, but didn't bother with the shirt before pulling me into his arms. I took a breath with my face pressed against his chest. A shudder ran through him.

"What's wrong?" My voice was muffled by his body.

He squeezed me tighter, then let go enough to look down at me. His eyes were still bright gold. "You disappeared."

I was missing something. "No. I went to my cousins' house…"

He brushed the hair from my face.

"I know I wasn't supposed to, but I had to go." I paused. His fear was slowly fading. "Why were you freaking out?"

"I…" He closed his eyes and let out a shaky breath. "I thought you died."

"What! Why would you think that?"

"All of a sudden, you were gone. I couldn't feel you through the bond. You weren't there anymore." He pulled me against his chest. "I thought you were dead," he said the words softly.

It wasn't just me that felt the bond disappear when I went through the gate. He'd felt it, too. Only he didn't know the reason.

I was a complete dumbass. I should've called him. This so wasn't winning me the Mate of the Year award.

"I'm sorry." I wrapped my arms around him. "Can't get rid of me that easily."

His hands tangled in my hair as he pulled me back into

his chest. "Just give me a second and I'll pull it back together." His heart was still racing. "I've had close calls, seen my life flash before my eyes, but nothing like what happened when our bond went dead. I saw our whole future disappear. All the things we'd never get to do. Getting married, having kids, going to see Paul van Dyk play…"

Married? Kids? I was going to pretend he didn't say that stuff. Instead, I reacted to the only thing on his list that I could mentally handle. "Paul van Dyk?"

"*Merde.*" He laughed. "That was supposed to be a surprise. For your birthday."

"Seriously?"

"Yeah. He's coming to Austin next weekend."

I grinned. "Best gift ever. I can't wait."

"It was kind of a selfish gift. I wanted to go dancing with you."

"Feel free to be that kind of selfish whenever you want." I pulled him down, and pressed my lips to his. He lifted me and I wrapped my legs around his waist. The feel of him against me was all-consuming. Heat raced through my body as my tongue brushed his. I squeezed my legs tighter around him and he nipped my lip.

I couldn't get close enough to him. It'd been like this since I first met him, and my obsession with him seemed to be getting worse instead of better.

Chris cleared his throat. "I'm still here. In case anyone was wondering."

I pulled back from Dastien, resting my forehead on his. "Way to kill the moment, jerk," I said to Chris, but I couldn't look away from Dastien. Not when his need to be with me filled our bond.

"*Je suis désole, mon amour.* I don't know what I'd do

without you."

I pressed a small kiss to his lips. "Babe. It was my fault. But I'm fine. We're fine."

He took a deep, shuddering breath. "Right." He closed his eyes, saying nothing, but he didn't need to. I could feel his love burning through me as the last of his panic slipped away.

"Let's go back," I said.

"Probably a good idea. I might have run out in the middle of teaching the freshmen a new maneuver."

I raised an eyebrow. "I'm sure the rumors will be flying." Everyone on campus knew that the only person to freak out the ever-steady Dastien Laurent was his mate.

Dastien set me down, and I hopped in the backseat. When I turned back to him, he was by the door, holding the T-shirt in his hand. I couldn't help but stare at his naked torso and the way his muscles moved as he shoved his arms into the gray cotton. He paused mid-motion, arms raised above his head, and looked at me.

I licked my lips and he grinned, dimples and all. Heat burned through my body. Both mine and his. It was too much. I was seconds away from jumping him.

"If you guys force me to chauffeur you while you make-out, I'm going to lose it," Chris said.

Dastien yelled something in quick French at Chris before getting in the car.

Chris laughed and said something back.

"In English, boys." Otherwise, I couldn't understand a word of what they were saying.

"I said that in the interest of those around you, maybe you can tone it down a notch," Chris said. "Or twenty."

My cheeks were on fire. "Shut up," I said as I hit the back of his seat.

Dastien slid across the seats and pulled me to him. "I'll never be upset that you're attracted to me. Don't be embarrassed."

"Easy for you to say. Jerk," I said. "Maybe don't be so hot next time. What was with that look? That pause with the shirt over your head? Jesus. I'm pretty sure my heart forgot to beat for a second. Are you trying to kill me?"

He laughed.

I shook my head. Guys were nuts. "Let's get out of here."

When Chris started driving, Dastien linked our hands together. "Did you feel our bond missing?"

"Yeah. I did." I winced. "But I brushed it aside as a side effect of being on their territory. Going through the gate onto their land wasn't exactly the most comfortable thing ever."

"You didn't think about calling me?"

"I'm sorry. The bond's there when I need it and otherwise, it feels a little snoopy to be checking on you all the time. Not to mention distracting. I'm having enough trouble in my classes as it is, thank you very much."

He smiled at me, but it wasn't exactly genuine. Man, I sucked.

"I was so focused on Meredith, I didn't even think that it'd affect you. Or that you'd notice." The look he gave me told me what he thought about that. "Sorry."

He squeezed my hand, letting me know it was forgiven, but I'd try not to mess that one up again.

"They warded their lands. Covens typically tell the alpha of the pack closest to them where they are so that any run-ins can be avoided, but no pack members actually go there. We always meet on neutral ground," Dastien said. "My best guess is that the ward either keeps people away from their compound or keeps intruders from escaping."

He looked at me, eyes flashing to gold for a second before going back to their normal amber. "It didn't even occur to me that you would go after we talked. I thought you went to class, and I felt you start to get agitated and the distance between us—that you were physically far away. I knew you'd gone there, and the bond disappeared and…" He trailed off and echoes of his terror rang strong through our bond. "I thought—"

I squeezed his hand, cutting him off. "I really am sorry. I honestly thought you wouldn't notice it, and moved on with what I was there to do. I wasn't planning on staying long." I paused as a thought hit me. "How much attention do you pay to our bond?"

Holy shit. My mate was blushing. I wasn't sure I'd ever seen him blush.

"Please tell me you're not going all creeper on me and looking in twenty-four-seven."

"*Creeper*? Really? You're my mate."

I widened my eyes. "What would you call it?"

"Keeping watch. You do have a tendency to get yourself into crazy situations."

"I don't do anything—"

Chris started laughing, but turned it into a cough when I hit the back of his seat.

"Barging in on the coven's compound first thing in the morning qualifies as a crazy situation."

He might have a point. I guessed that I did stick my nose in a few places it didn't belong. In my defense, if I hadn't stuck my nose in, bad things would've gone down in the pack. But before I met Dastien, I totally stayed out of trouble. "My life was totally normal until I met you, buddy."

"Says the girl who had visions whenever she touched anything. Yeah, I don't buy that for a second."

I smacked his arm. "Not funny."

Chris chuckled from the front seat. Great. I was getting laughed at by both guys in my own car.

"Come on. It was a little funny," Dastien said.

I tried to keep from laughing, but ended up grinning anyway. I leaned into him and he wrapped his arm around my shoulder.

"Did you call me 'buddy'?" He murmured as he brushed a kiss on my head.

"I may have, but that's beside the point," I muttered mostly to myself.

Chris cleared his throat. "How's Meredith?"

Any laughter I felt died.

"The same," Dastien said. "She's knocked out, and we'll try to keep her that way for as long as possible. Did you learn anything?"

"Oh, they'll break the curse. But only if I let them put the same curse on me and move there indefinitely."

Dastien growled.

Whoops. I probably shouldn't have said that aloud, even if it was bothering me. I would've been fine if they wanted me to stay and learn their ways maybe once a week, but foregoing the pack and letting her curse me—no way.

I could almost see the steam coming from Dastien's ears as rage boiled along our bond.

Still, if I was going to have an equal relationship with Dastien, then keeping things from him—especially something like this—wasn't the best call. If the situation were reversed, I'd want to know. "Claudia gave me some books, but unless I submit, and I won't—"

"Damned right," Chris said.

"*And* I won't," I said again, talking over Chris' mutterings. "They can't—or won't—do anything else to help Meredith." I started to climb across the seats to get back in the front passenger side, but Dastien stopped me.

"We're still moving." His deep voice rumbled with worry.

"So? I'm a werewolf and pretty much unbreakable, even if Chris wrecks." I brushed a kiss on his forehead, and stepped over him, into the front seat. Just because he worried, didn't mean I'd let him coddle me.

"Don't wreck," Dastien said to Chris.

"Thanks for the advice, dude. I'll do my best."

I snorted.

"Seatbelt," Dastien said as soon as I sat.

Seriously? The guy needed to calm down. I was fine. I would stay fine. It was Meredith we had to worry about. I reached to the floorboard and pulled the three books out of my bag.

The first one was two inches thick with a navy blue cover and embossed silver letters on the front that spelled out *McCondry's Basics of Magic, Spells & Curses*. The second book was small, about the size of a pocket guide. The cover was a dark brown and very worn-in, but it didn't have a title. I opened the little book and a page fell out.

This book could seriously use a rebinding.

I placed the page back in and read the handwritten, tiny print. Different people had scrawled all over the page, crossing things out, making replacements, and underlining words. I wondered who, and how many witches, had owned the book before me, but that didn't matter. The only thing that mattered was that I had it. From what I could tell, these were actual potions. The boil-things-in-a-pot kind.

The last book was the newest. The hardcover had a glossy finish. *A Practical Guide to Witchcraft* was printed above the image of a girl standing with an odd-looking chemistry set. The spine cracked with newness when I opened it. I quickly flipped through the pages since I didn't have to turn them as gingerly as I did the others. It looked like my metaphysics text, complete with exercises after every chapter, but from a *bruja* perspective instead of a werewolf one.

Weird. Were there even enough witches to warrant such a book? "How many witches are there?"

"A lot. Nearly a hundred times the current amount of wolves," Chris said.

"What? Seriously?" I twisted to look at Dastien.

He nodded. "Almost every culture has some sort of witchcraft in it. To some it's so watered down that it's more like a normal religion and not all of them have powers. But there's a pretty solid number of covens that do. Besides the coven here, the strongest ones are in Peru and Mexico. And the one in India is pretty good, too."

"And the Egyptian one," Chris said. "That one's badass. But yours is really well known."

And they were thinking about taking on the pack. Being that grossly outnumbered didn't sit well with me. I'd have to see what I could do about mending things between the pack and the coven before the situation with Luciana got out of control.

I flipped through some more pages. If I was a betting girl, which I wasn't, I'd bet this was the one that Luciana and the others didn't want me to have.

"Anything good?" Chris asked.

"It's too soon to tell. I'll need help going through

everything, but maybe. If there's a way to fix to what's going on with Meredith, we'll find it in here."

"Can I see that one?" Dastien asked. I handed the newest book to him, and went back to the one with no title. Something about it called to me.

Unfortunately, every word was gobbledygook.

Rise to the west, and the soul to the east...Light the candles clockwise to find the one you seek.

I understood the words and maybe the sentiment behind them, but I didn't quite get what they were accomplishing.

By the time Chris pulled into the St. Ailbe's parking lot, I knew more about spells, but none of it was exactly helpful. Hopefully one of the other books would be marginally less confusing.

I slipped the books into my bag and hopped down from the car. Chris tossed me the keys, and I caught them. A few weeks ago, this would've been a shocker—my coordination used to be less than fantastic—but being a Were was good for some things. Dastien walked so close beside me that our arms brushed. If it'd been anyone else, I'd tell them to take a step to the side, but with Dastien, it was comforting.

When we got to the edge of the parking lot, Adrian, Shannon, and Dr. Gonzales were waiting. Adrian and Shannon were the other two people—besides Dastien, Meredith, and Chris—that I hung out with.

I was really glad to see Adrian. Since he had more experience with the magic stuff, my first mission was going to be pulling him from class, but since he was here, we could dig right in.

Dr. Gonzales stepped forward first.

Oh no... My heart stuttered. "Is Meredith—"

"No change."

I shoved my shaking hands in my pockets. "That's good." I guessed.

"We were more concerned with you. When Dastien ran off and we realized you were missing, we thought you might be coming back injured." Dr. Gonzales patted her black messenger bag. "But you look fine."

"We had a little scare, but she's okay." Dastien put his arm around my shoulders and pulled me to his side. "I might not ever be fine again, but Tessa's snarky as ever."

"Shut up." I elbowed him.

Shannon's eyes were red, making her green eyes bright. She tucked a piece of her curly red hair behind her ear. "Did you get Meredith sorted?" Her sing-song-y Irish accent rang clear. Shannon still had a thing for Dastien and it'd been tense between us. This was the first time she'd directly spoken to me in a week.

"Maybe. It was worth the trip." I paused. "I tried to talk them into breaking the curse, but Luciana won't unless I let her curse me and move in with the coven."

Shannon narrowed her eyes. She'd probably like it if I accepted Luciana's terms.

"That's never going to happen." I left no room for argument. "Anyway...I got some books from my cousins. They said the books might be helpful, so I'm hoping that's code for *definitely* helpful. If all of you wouldn't mind looking through them with me, that would be awesome."

"I have to go back to teaching, and you need to eat," Dastien said.

"I'll eat later."

"Tessa."

I sighed. I wanted to keep working on this, but needed to stay level-headed, which made eating a priority. "Okay.

I'll go by the common room and grab some sandwiches, and then we can meet in the admin building in a few?"

The others nodded and Dastien agreed. With that figured out, I made my way across campus. I wanted to run to the common area, but made myself walk. It was a fast walk, but I was keeping it together.

I was banking on these books, because Plan B was not an option.

But if the magic doesn't work…

I silenced my inner doubt. It would work. I'd spend every second I had to make sure Meredith was okay.

That was the only option.

Chapter Six

After grabbing food, I reconvened with Shannon, Adrian, and Chris on the first floor of the administration building. Shannon led the way to a conference room. Most of the space was taken up by a long rectangular table surrounded by chairs. A buffet table in the back held a stack of yellow legal pads, a cup of pens and highlighters, and a case of water bottles. Maybe this was where they held the pack meetings? For some reason, I'd pictured them taking place in the woods around a campfire, like where we voted whether or not to keep Imogene in the pack, but maybe they were usually more conventional than that.

We spread out around half the table. I sat on one side with Adrian and Shannon across from me. Chris took a seat at the head. I took the three books out of my bag and placed them on the tabletop. "This is what we've got to work with."

Chris reached behind him and grabbed a legal pad for each of us, then put the cup with pens and highlighters in the center of the table.

Adrian snatched up the nameless brown book. "I can't believe they actually gave you this one." His dark brown eyes were wide with wonder as he looked through it.

With all the scribbling, I knew the book was different, but I wasn't sure what that meant. "What's the deal? Why is it all handwritten?"

"It's a Book of Shadows."

Whoa. I'd heard of those. Only because I watched *Charmed*. It was a guilty pleasure.

On the show, the Book of Shadows was a family's spell book handed down from generation to generation. "I didn't know people had those in real life."

He carefully closed the book and ran his hand over the cover. "Yep. Every family has different spells, different ways of doing things. At least that's what I was always told. It gets passed on to the oldest child from each generation."

That didn't make sense. "Newsflash. I'm not the oldest in my family. Axel is. And I'm pretty sure Claudia and Raphael are older than me, too."

Adrian shrugged. "I guess I'm wrong. Maybe it's not the oldest, but the most powerful?"

I moved uncomfortably in my seat. If that were true, then Claudia had taken a huge risk by giving me the book. No wonder Raphael had been against it.

Adrian opened the book again and Shannon scooted closer to him to read.

I started with Chapter One of mine. It had great information on the basics of witchcraft, explaining how magic was a test of one's will and faith. But none of that specifically helped Meredith. When I had a few days, I'd start at the beginning, but for now, I flipped to the back of the book.

The index had an entry for "breaking curses." That

sounded much more applicable.

I started reading it and things got interesting. For all intents and purposes, the book implied that messing with anyone else's curses was a bad idea. Apparently it caused 'adverse effects,' which included illness, wasting diseases, and painful death.

That sounded like a bunch of not cool.

I scribbled down "NEVER try breaking a curse" on my notepad. Not that I needed the note to remind me, but it was good to keep in mind if I ever got desperate.

The chapter went into some gruesome details— pictures included—of people who had tried and failed to break a curse. At the end was a note.

Although it is inadvisable to break another's curse or spell, counteracting it can be achieved. If the caster's will and faith be stronger than those of the original caster, then the effects of the curse or spell may be lessened or even overridden.

The relief I felt was tangible. Now, all I needed to do was find a spell to counteract the curse on Meredith.

I flipped back to the index and searched for anything that sounded helpful. The way I figured, there were two real options. Breaking the curse wasn't one of them. We either needed to put Meredith's wolf back to sleep or we needed a spell strong enough to override the original curse, which would release her wolf. Everyone else at the table was all about finding the latter, but getting Meredith's wolf to chill seemed like the safest option. Then this new spell wouldn't have to be stronger than Luciana's spell or even override it. It just had to work alongside it.

I lost all track of time. The scratch of my highlighter against the glossy finish of the crisp textbook pages and the scraping sound of pens against paper filled the room.

Occasionally Adrian and Shannon whispered to each other about possible spells, but I tuned them out. I was determined to find answers.

After a while, my eyes were watering and my back was stiff. I stood and stretched, my joints popping as I leaned back. "Do you see anything in the books for a spell about either releasing or quieting a wolf?"

"Shannon and I found a couple possible spells to try," Adrian said.

That was promising. "Chris?" I said.

He was reading the blue book, his nose nearly pressed into the spine. He held up a finger.

Okay. He needed more time. "Well, mine is about as useless as meta class." I had to take metaphysics with the freshmen. The class tried, and, in my opinion, failed miserably to explain magic in scientific terms. "It's got all these theories about how magic works, which is great, but no actual spells that could be helpful." I sighed.

"What does it say about breaking spells?" Shannon asked.

I flipped through the pages to find a passage that I'd marked. "The meat of it boils down to this passage. 'The abilities of one witch will determine the abilities of each work of magic.' It has a bunch of junkola after that and then the next part is good. 'The longevity of the work is determined by the strength of the will enforcing said work. The potency and sustainability of a work can be partly determined by the strength of the witch's will. Most works of magic wear out in time, but when breaking a particular work, the abilities of the caster must be weighed against those of the breaker.'" I glanced up from the book. "So if I want to break the spell, then I have to have stronger willpower than Luciana. If I don't, the whole thing could backfire."

Now it was time to share my crazy idea.

"We basically need Meredith's wolf to not fight her anymore, right? But we're thinking like wolves—about freeing Meredith from the spell. If we can't do that safely, then why not try to put her wolf back to sleep? We wouldn't have to worry about anything backfiring then. Or who's stronger than who."

"Might not be such a horrible idea," Chris said. "I was reading about the dangers of breaking a spell, too, but this one says it differently. Basically, if you want to break the spell that she put on Meredith, then all you have to do is want it more. But it's hard to quantify how badly someone wants something. It's a huge risk. Do you think you want to break it more than Luciana wants to keep it?"

I slammed my book closed. "How the hell should I know?"

Chris rocked back in his chair. He ran his fingers through his blond wavy hair, making it fro-out a little. "Well, if you try to break it by will, and fail, then you could end up making her much worse. Not to mention that it could rub off on you, too. You could get sick in the process."

Great. I didn't want to make Meredith's curse any worse than it already was, but I had to do something. Breaking the curse was still the option I liked the most, but it might not be the safest.

"How was the other book?" I asked Shannon and Adrian, stalling.

"We found a couple contenders that could maybe break a spell."

Nice. I leaned toward them. "And?"

"Aaaand I'm not sure where we'd find some of the

components for some of these potions," Adrian said as he tapped his pen on his notepad.

"One of them even calls for the blood of the caster," Shannon said.

Luciana had to give me her blood? Yeah, that would never happen. "Not in a million years would she give us her blood."

We were quiet afterwards, each of us lost in our own thoughts.

I would've felt better about trying a spell if I could talk to Donovan. He knew more about dealing with this than any of us. It would be nice to get his opinion before attempting anything, but that wasn't going to happen.

Screw it. I wasn't going to try anything that would be even more dangerous for Meredith. "As much as you all might not like it, I think we drop the idea of breaking the curse, and instead focus on finding one that will work alongside the curse to quiet her wolf."

Shannon's face was red as she yelled a stream of curses at me. I sat there quietly, letting them vent their anger and frustration. When I had enough I stood up. "Stop." The word had enough power to get them to instantly shut up.

"Here's the problem. Anything we try to counter the spell with has big repercussions. Meredith is extremely sick. We cannot make it worse for her or she'll die. Something made her wolf fight against her curse. The two parts that make up Meredith are at war after three years of being totally fine. So, we put the wolf back to sleep and she should go back to being fine." I sat back down. "Maybe one day we can find a way to break the curse for good," I said softly. "But right now, none of us know enough to fix this. So, we do our best to keep Meredith alive."

"I agree." Chris slid his chair back from the table. "It's

our best shot."

"No! I refuse to believe that. It's because she's one of them." The disgust was clear in Shannon's voice. "Look at her. She hasn't even accepted her own wolf. Why would she help one of us?"

I growled. My wolf surged faster than ever before. "This isn't about getting Meredith's wolf back. It's about keeping her alive." I slammed my hand on the table, and it groaned. Anger was not my friend right now, but I couldn't rein it back. "You're too close-minded to see what's best for her."

"What's best is making her whole." Shannon spat the words at me as she leaned over the table. "Her wolf wants out, and we should be helping to free her. Once that happens, she'll be okay."

"Don't you get it? Trying to mess around with that curse could kill her!" Fur rippled along my arms. "Shit. Not now."

Shannon pointed at me and turned to Adrian. "Look at that. Her wolf is begging to be set free and she's too scared to let it. It's unnatural. And she'd have us imprison one of ours. I'll not stand for it."

I turned my back to them as I tried to get myself under control. My stomach burned with the need to change. My knuckles popped.

I will not change. I will not change. I will not change.

I ignored their yelling. I knew I was right. It was the only way.

Slowly, my wolf settled down. I breathed a sigh of relief. Today was not a good day to change.

"As much as I hate to say it, Tess has a point," Adrian said. "But maybe if we knew what happened to her, what the spell or curse was, then we'd know how to calm her wolf better."

I spun around. "Does anyone know what happened?"

Shannon stayed quiet, while Chris and Adrian shook their heads.

Interesting. I wondered what Shannon was hiding.

"Well, we can't let Dr. Gonzales wake her up," I said. "The sedatives won't work for long anyway."

Chris bounced a pencil on the table. The tap-tap-tap made me more on edge than I already was, if that was even possible. I ripped the pencil from his hand, snapped it in half, and threw it across the room. Wooden splinters rained down on the gray shag carpeting.

Everyone in the room froze.

"Holy shit. I'm sorry. I don't know why I did that." I'd reached the point where I was acting without thinking. My control was seriously slipping and I hadn't even noticed it. The wolf inside me was gaining the upper hand, and that couldn't happen. I sat heavily in my chair.

"It's fine. I didn't realize I was tapping my pencil." Chris shrugged it off like it was no big deal. To them, maybe it wasn't. To me, it was.

"It was the sound, but God—I've never just done that. It was incredibly rude. I'm so sorry." My wolf wasn't conflicted about it. Something was annoying me and she stopped it.

Oh no. I was starting to realize what my wolf wanted.

"This might be a crazy idea…" Chris started, then shook his head.

Focusing on Meredith meant I didn't have to deal with the whole wolf thing. I waited for Chris to speak up, but he didn't. "Spill it."

"I know you can get visions and stuff, but can you dig around in someone's mind?"

The thought of doing that turned my stomach. Messing around in someone's head seemed a shade darker than anything I ever wanted to do. It was worse than snooping around someone's closet or medicine cabinet. Everyone had secrets and memories that they'd rather not talk about. What I saw, even when it was something little, was extremely personal, and I felt exactly what they felt. Saw what they saw. To dig around in multiple memories, hoping to run across the right one...that seemed far from kosher.

How far would I go to save Meredith?

Apparently pretty far, because I was seriously thinking about giving this plan a shot. "I've never tried. I spent my whole life trying to avoid getting visions, so forcing one from someone wasn't even on my radar. But getting a specific vision of an event...I don't know. I could try. You think it'd help?"

"Yes," Adrian said. "If you could figure out how she got cursed, then maybe we'd have a better shot at undoing it."

"I guess it's worth a try." I just hoped Meredith wouldn't mind me messing around in her head.

Chapter Seven

I opened the conference room door and walked straight into Dastien. He grasped my shoulders as I stumbled back a step.

"What's up?" I asked.

He'd changed from the sweats into his usual jeans and T-shirt, but his eyes still held worry. "I was going to ask you the same thing. I felt you go a little…out of control." He squeezed my shoulders once before letting go. "What's going on?"

I didn't even know how to answer that question. I was feeling on edge. That said, I'd been feeling on edge since my run-in with Luciana. Being anxious wasn't unusual for me, but today was over the top. I'd nearly shifted twice already, and it wasn't even dinnertime. To say that I felt uneasy was an extreme understatement, and I didn't like it at all. I used to be even-keeled. With my visions, I had to be able to roll with whatever was going on, but now I was a mess.

"I'm thinking of doing something that I'm not exactly sure is a super fantastic idea," I said, taking the easy road out rather than discussing my wolf for the one-millionth time.

"We're going to the infirmary to see if Tess can see what happened when Meredith was cursed," Shannon said.

Who knew she was such a little tattletale? Not that I wouldn't tell Dastien, but it would've been nice to ask his opinion myself. I gave her a less-than-friendly look, but Shannon didn't look the least bit sorry.

"Are you sure that's something you want to try?" Dastien asked.

"No. But I don't see a ton of alternatives." I shrugged. "Unless you've managed to get a hold of Donovan?"

"No. Not yet. But I left a message with his hotel in Cusco." He ran his fingertips down my arm before taking my hand. Our bond strengthened. The first time I'd felt it, it was like a jolt of electricity. Now it was like a warming hum.

Thinking about our bond made me remember something. "The pack has a bond, too. Right?"

"Yeah," Adrian said. "Of course."

"Can you feel other people in the pack?"

"Sort of." Shannon stepped a little too close to Dastien. "Depends on where you are in the pack hierarchy."

I tried to ignore my annoyance with her. "So why don't you send a warning via the pack bond or something? You're high enough up." I asked Dastien.

"I wish I could, but only the appointed Alpha of each pack can find members of their own pack—which I'm not. I'm only standing in for Michael while he's away. Even if I were the official Alpha here, Donovan would be out of my league. Only another member of the Seven could find him."

Well, there went my genius idea. "That does make things more complicated."

"Can I have a moment with her? Alone?" Dastien asked our friends.

"I'll meet you in Meredith's infirmary room," I said.

Once they were gone, Dastien closed the door. "Are you okay?"

"Yeah." It was a total lie, but everything would hold until Meredith was better.

"You're saying one thing, but I can sense that you're feeling another."

I let go of his hand. Sometimes I liked to keep my emotions to myself. Having someone know what was simmering under the surface was unsettling. But he got a pass this time. I didn't have the time or energy to try and explain what privacy meant to me.

I crossed my arms, trying to let my annoyance go. "I *am* okay to some degree, but it's all relative, you know?"

He pulled out two chairs, and faced them together. "Sit. Let's get you calm again before you go try this thing with Meredith."

That was a fantastic idea. I couldn't afford to lose control of my wolf. I'd nearly attacked Luciana this morning, and that wasn't acceptable. Now I was an inch away from totally snapping on my friends.

After the Tribunal, things would be easier. Or so I hoped. But until then, I needed to be on my A game all the time. Today it felt like I was on my C-minus game at best.

He sat in the other chair. "So, I'll ask it again. How are you doing?"

"Not great. I'm totally on edge about everything. I'm wasting time talking to you and that's kind of pissing me off—"

"You're not wasting time," he said, interrupting me. He frowned. "I hope you know that this might not be fixable. You can't control everything. You can't save everyone."

I chewed on my lip. This wasn't what I wanted to hear. Not at all. "I don't want to save everyone. Just Meredith."

"I know, *cherie.* I know." He leaned toward me and placed his hand on my knee. The scent that I'd come to know as his—forest and something a little spicy that was just him—comforted me. "Are you sure you want to do this? It wasn't that long ago that you wanted to get rid of your visions entirely."

I slouched in the chair as I thought about the truth in his words. "I did, but this is different."

"Then why are you so conflicted about it?"

It all came down to one thing. Privacy. It was something that I cherished, and as someone who got a lot of crap for intruding on other people's memories, I knew how much others valued theirs. "It feels immoral. Like it's ethically shitty of me to even consider doing it. But I don't see any other way."

"She wouldn't mind. If she were awake, she'd let you in. So, I don't know why you're beating yourself up."

I wasn't so sure of that. Meredith liked her privacy more than most. And, if I was being honest with myself, it wasn't just that. I didn't like being sucked into other people's memories. It wasn't fun for me. I'd already lost touch with every aspect of reality that I held true. I wasn't sure how much more I could take.

"Will it make you feel better or worse if I go with you?"

Would it make me look weak to need him to hold my hand? Probably. Did I care? Not really. Having him in the same room centered me. "That would actually be great. You don't mind?"

"*Cherie.*" I grinned at his look of exasperation. "What wouldn't I do for you?"

"I don't know." But I was starting to think that there really wasn't much.

He shook his head. "It'd be nice to have a little bit of an upper hand on something in this relationship." The words were a little mumbled.

I grabbed his shirt and pulled him toward me. "Thank you," I said when our lips were almost touching.

"For what?"

"For being you."

The sight of his dimpled grin made my heart race. He went the final little bit, and our lips touched. I wanted to breathe him in. His heart pounded as I ran my hands under his shirt.

He bit my lip. "You're playing with something dangerous."

"Dangerous might not be so bad."

His eyes flashed golden for a split second. "Not yet. After the ceremony, then yes." He took a breath. "*Merde*, Tess. You're making it really hard."

"That's what she said."

His whole body shook as he laughed. "I walked into that one."

"Yup." I stood, and straightened my shirt. "Let's go see Meredith."

I pulled him out of the chair and grabbed my bag, tucking the books safely inside.

***

The infirmary was on the third floor of the admin building. I knew it well. When I first arrived at St. Ailbe's

I'd stayed in one of the infirmary's rooms, but I'd been pretty out of it. Waking up with some crazy memories of being in a cage had made me jump out of the window. It probably wasn't my smartest move.

Then I'd gotten bit by a nasty vamp and found myself back again. The infirmary was becoming my third home. One I never wanted, but that was life as a werewolf. At least that was my life as a werewolf.

Meredith's room was like any of the other rooms in the infirmary—tiny. One window let in a bit of light. A twin bed took up the center, and cabinets lined the wall to the left of the bed.

A cushy brown leather chair took up the corner in the right side of the room. Shannon sniffled, crying softly as she slouched forward in it. Her face was pale, and her freckles stood out in stark contrast. Adrian sat next to her, his arm around her shoulders. A look of resignation was visible in his eyes.

Chris stood at the side of the bed, holding Meredith's hand. He was the only one of us who hadn't seen her yet. He met my gaze. "It's worse than I thought."

She seemed peaceful as she lay there. Her features were relaxed while the drugs kept her in a deep, coma-like sleep, but her cheekbones stood out too much to mistake her for anything other than sick. Her skin had taken on a pale yellowish-green tint. Dark circles lined her eyes. It wasn't just the way she looked physically, but the way she smelled. Slightly sour. Slightly chemically, possibly from metabolizing the drugs. An IV ran into her arm, keeping a steady stream going into her system.

I stepped up to the bed. She'd been fine last night. Happy, glowing, and loving life. And now, she was at death's door. What the hell happened?

Heels clicked down the hallway toward us. As far as I knew there was only one person at St. Ailbe's who wore stilettos.

"She's wasting away," I said to Dr. Gonzales.

She stood in the doorway, letting us surround our friend. "There's not much I can do. I'm pumping nutrients into her body, but a werewolf's metabolism is incredibly rapid."

I leaned down to whisper in her ear. "You stay alive. Give me a chance to fix it." I rubbed my hands on my jeans. Doing this with an audience wasn't going to be fun. "I'm not sure how long this might take or if it'll even work."

"Take your time," Adrian said. "We'll wait."

Chris left the room abruptly. I thought he was giving me space and maybe the others would take the hint, but he came back a second later with a chair. He placed it behind me and motioned to it. "There. Just in case you need it."

"Thanks." I sat down and scooted it right up to Meredith's bed. I took a deep breath, and told myself to relax. This was going to work.

Dastien stood beside me. I grabbed his hand, trusting that he would keep his own walls up so that he wouldn't give me anything of his to 'see,' and blocked out everything else in the room.

I leaned forward. "Show me when Luciana cursed you. Show me what happened," I said before putting my other hand in hers. It only took a second before my surroundings gave way to the vision.

I was in a room done in pink and white. A little girl with white-blonde hair played with a dollhouse. She whispered as she moved the dolls around.

"Nerd. Are you talking to your dolls again?" A tall blond teenage guy came into the room.

"I wouldn't have to if I had someone to play with."

"Where is everyone?"

"Matt's at soccer. Micah and Miles went for a run. Mom and Dad are out."

Whoa. Her parents really had a thing for M-names.

"So it's just you and me?"

"Yup."

"Alright, well I'm not playing with dolls. Let's go."

Meredith's young face shined as she grinned and raced across the room to him.

"Meredith," I said into the vision. "Show me what happened. Please."

Light flared. I couldn't see anything. I heard distant voices echoing along the white expanse.

Someone was sobbing. A girl. Meredith.

And then, just as quickly as it started, it faded.

A wolf whined.

The white dimmed until I could make out shadows. Colors. I blinked, and suddenly I was in a field. Bluebonnets blanketed the ground. Wolves ran by me. A light brown one caught up with a smaller white one, and nipped at her tail. The sight of the two wolves playing made me smile.

This wasn't what I needed to see.

"Please, Meredith. Show me what happened when you were cursed. Show me what I need to see," I said in the vision.

The blinding white light came again. This time, I shielded my eyes with my hand.

The sobbing came again. And the sadness. Just a taste of it, and then gone.

Familiar sounds surrounded me. Utensils clinking against plates. People chatting. Two people—girls—were *yelling. I peeked through my fingers.*

I was in the cafeteria at St. Ailbe's. Meredith and Imogene stood nose to nose. Shouting at each other.

"You think you can say that kind of shit about me and get away with it," Meredith yelled.

Shannon grabbed Meredith's arm, pulling her away from Imogene as Mr. Dawson came running. Before anyone could stop her, Meredith reached down into the plate piled high with loaded mashed potatoes. Her fingers sunk into them, and she threw them in Imogene's face.

Everyone in the cafeteria froze for a second before a full-on food fight broke out.

I laughed. Hard. That was the best. I couldn't wait for Meredith to wake up. We so needed to talk about that.

As fun as these images were, I wasn't seeing anything of consequence. How was I supposed to get one specific image? I needed the scene with Luciana.

"Show me what happened with Luciana," I said to Meredith. She didn't acknowledge me at all in the vision, but the light flared again.

The sobbing came again. Louder this time. Beating against me in the empty white canvas.

As the sobbing slowed, the next vision came into view. The cabinets were the first thing I could make out. Then countertops. A stove.

I was in a kitchen. It was huge, bigger than the whole downstairs of my house in California.

Meredith sat at the counter, and her mother stood across from her.

Her mom looked like she'd stepped out of a magazine. White-blond hair hung in perfect silky curls down her back. The printed wrap dress wasn't inherently sexy, but somehow, it showed off her curves. With the wedge sandals, she had to have been over six feet tall.

Now I knew where Meredith got her looks.

"You need to find a mate, honey. It's time."

Meredith shook her head. "I can't, Mom. Even if I liked any of the guys at school, I'm cursed."

"It's your duty to the pack to find a mate. I don't care who you pick, but pick someone. And soon. Do you understand me?"

"Yes, Mom. I understand."

This was messed up. Didn't Meredith's mother care about what her daughter wanted at all?

Her mother passed her a binder.

"What's this?"

"Possible matches."

Yuck. She had an actual binder of men.

"All of the potential mates in there have been advised of your situation and are willing to take you on as is."

Jesus. As is? What was she, a car?

"Meredith!" I yelled. "Show me something relevant. I need to know how I can help you! Please!"

The light came so fast that I couldn't block my eyes. No sobbing to warn me this time.

I blinked, trying to make the spots go away. And then I realized that it wasn't spots. I was outside somewhere, lying on the ground and staring at the sun.

I stood up as my sight slowly started to come back.

Meredith was lying on a blanket in the courtyard in the center of the St. Ailbe's buildings. A pile of magazines was abandoned on her right. One was open to a page filled with purses.

Donovan stood over her. His dark wavy hair was tucked behind his ears. His blue eyes shone with a touch of wolf. He wasn't pissed. Or even upset. But hurt. I couldn't feel what he was feeling, but I could tell from the slight frown on his face. The way he shoved his hands in his pockets.

"I can't. You have to go," Meredith said. She crossed her arms and scowled at him. She looked mad but she wasn't. She was sad. Really sad. It made my heart ache.

He knelt by her but she rolled on her side, giving him her back.

"Please, don't do this," he said.

I could feel her pain as if it were my own. She didn't want to say that. She didn't want to hurt him, but she didn't have a choice.

"It's what's best," she continued. Donovan couldn't see her face, but I could. Tears fell freely down her cheeks, but her voice was steady. "You don't really want me. Not like this. And I can't...I won't..." She took a breath. "I won't be a burden to you."

"You're not a burden. I'll not have you say that." He rolled her on her back. "Ach. No. Please, don't cry." His Irish accent thickened with his emotion.

God. This was not something I wanted to see. This was such an invasion of privacy.

"So you do have feelings for me."

My heart was breaking for these two. They should be together. It didn't have to be this way.

Meredith squeezed her eyes shut. "It doesn't matter what I feel. You're one of the Seven, and I'm broken."

He sat down beside her, cupping her face in his hand, wiping her tears away with his thumbs. "You're not broken."

"Yes, I am. My wolf...she's gone. That means I'm broken."

"She's not broken. She's right there." He tapped her

sternum. "I can feel her for myself."

Meredith's eyes opened, and hope filled her face.

"If broken's how you feel, then we'll get it sorted."

A car honked in the distance.

"I have to go, but I'll be back as soon as I can. It isn't over. You're mine, and I've waited too long for you to give up over something silly." He pressed a kiss to her forehead. "Goodbye for now, a ghrá."

Meredith didn't say anything as he left. When he was gone, she started crying. Gut-wrenching sobs.

That's what I'd been hearing.

Still in the vision, I knelt by her. "Meredith."

She didn't make a move.

I moved forward to shake her, but my hands went right through her.

Damn it.

"Meredith!" I'd never tried to see something other than what someone wanted to show me. I needed her subconscious to wake up enough to show me what I needed to see. "Meredith! Listen to me!" I backed power in the command. "I need to see what happened. I need to know how you got cursed! Show me!"

Instead of seeing the light, the vision rewound. Everything happened in reverse until Donovan stood over her again. Then it replayed. The same heartbreaking scene.

Meredith was torturing herself.

"No! Meredith! Stop this!" I pulled more power through Dastien. "I need to know how to help you. Please, show me what Luciana did so that I can try to fix it."

She turned, just a little, and looked at me.

"Focus, Meredith. What happened with the curse, Meredith? What did she do to you?"

The scene rewound.

Christ. This wasn't working.

I watched it unfold again. I yelled at her. Throwing my power around, trying to get her to listen, but nothing worked.

Why was she showing it to me so many times? What was I missing?

When the scene unfolded for a third time, I got a little crazy. My wolf started rising as the need to change burned my skin. I felt power roll through me from my bond with Dastien. I knew it was meant to help stabilize me, but it gave me an idea.

I took it and threw his power at the vision. "Meredith! Stop it! I know he's your mate, but we can't get to him. We put out word, but he's not back yet."

I wasn't sure if I should give up yet. She could hear me. I knew she could. She kept changing the scene every time I asked. But now she was stuck on this.

I had to try and reason with her. Sensing the pack beyond Dastien, I pulled even more power. "You're so sick, Meredith. You're going to die if I don't find a way to stop this. I need you to show me what happened with Luciana. Please. Show me. I won't judge you. I only want to help!"

"What're ya yelling about?" *I heard Donovan's far away voice.*

"Donovan?"

"Tessa?"

The same memory kept playing, but I could hear Donovan's voice over it. Barely. "How?"

"Through the bond I have with my mate, but it's a weak bond and can't maintain this type of pack link for long. What are you doing in her memories? And why is she knocked out? Who drugged her?" *Donovan's voice was getting growly at the end.*

I took a deep breath. Getting across the right bits of information was key. "She's been sedated. Her wolf is awake and Meredith's been cursed not to change, so her body's fighting itself. We're trying to find a way to break the curse, but I don't know what to do. I need to know what happened, but she won't show me."

"That's why she said she was broken. Shite. I woke her damned wolf up by poking at her. Why did no one tell me this? How could I not know?" He muttered the questions.

I grabbed more power and channeled it into the bond between Meredith and Donovan. "What do I do? Tell me what I can do to help."

"I'm on my way back."

"Where are you?"

"In the Andes."

Middle-of-nowhere, Peru. It was going to take days for him to get back. "You're too far. She won't last. Can you make her show me what I need to see?"

"I wish I could, but I can't. If she's sleeping hard enough to not wake from what you're pushing through her, then she's been put in a stasis and I won't bring her out of it. It's what's keeping her alive." He was quiet for a moment.

Anxiety built in me. I pushed more power, hoping I wasn't draining Dastien too much.

"Ach. I see. Thank God you're there. I can't fix this, but you can. It's all you. And I might not get there in time to help you either. I'm running now, but it'll take me a day to get to the city. I'll be on the first flight out, but…Christ. I shouldn't have left her."

Donovan was taking too much time. I shoved more power at him. "Donovan! I don't know what to do! How do I fix this?"

"You need to help her wolf," his voice was softer. I

91

could barely hear him. "You're going to have to merge witchcraft—"

I slammed back into my own mind. Dastien's panic and worry flowed through my soul, making my head swim.

"What happened?" My voice slurred. It slowly registered that I was flat on my back. The cold floor burned against me. What happened to the chair?

A line a sweat ran from my hairline. I opened my eyes and immediately regretted it. The lights were too bright. I flung my hand over my eyes as I moaned. "Way too bright. It's killing my head."

There was some whispering and rustling around the room. The shrill sound of flimsy metal rang out as the blinds to the small window were drawn.

Someone was coughing and moaning.

"Give me a blanket or a pillow or something," Dastien said.

The sound of cabinets opening and closing felt like gunshots to my head. Dastien's scent enveloped me as he eased my head onto a pillow. "How are you feeling, *cherie*?"

I took a quiet assessment of myself. "Honestly, I feel like shit. Why do I feel so terrible?"

"You're nearly completely energy-drained. You started out by putting all your power into whatever you were doing, and then I fed you my power, and you took that. But then you took from the whole pack. I don't know what you were doing there, but you were draining us all. We were fine with it, but when Meredith's heart beat started slowing, we realized you were pulling from her too."

Oh God. "Is she okay?"

"No. She's coughing up blood in her sleep," Shannon answered.

Fear coursed through me. "Fuck. I didn't know what I was doing."

"We figured," Adrian said. "It didn't matter what you were seeing, we had to stop it. She can't take much more."

I wanted to scream and cry, but couldn't muster the energy. "I was talking to Donovan—"

"That's impossible," Shannon said.

I didn't have the patience to deal with her. "It's completely possible if they're true mates, which they are." My words were clipped.

The reaction was much what I thought it'd be. Silence. And then everyone was talking all at once.

I moaned. "Can everyone please shut the hell up? My head is killing me. Worst migraine ever."

Chris snorted. "I'd say. You were harnessing so much through the bonds, it's a miracle you're not a vegetable."

"Did he say anything helpful?" Adrian asked softly. Bless him.

Dastien massaged my temples, and some of the pain dissipated.

"Not really." Talking made me nauseated, so I tried to keep it limited. "He's far, but on his way now. He said I'd have to merge witchcraft with something else. I was pulled out before he could say. Any ideas?" I tried to sit up, but started to fall.

"Whoa." Dastien caught me before I could hit the ground. "I got you." He pulled me onto his lap. He scooted so he was leaning against the cabinets. I leaned against him listening to his steady heartbeat.

"What's wrong with me?"

Dastien brushed my hair back from my face, and

pressed a kiss to my head. "When I said you were drained, I meant it. It's going to take a little bit before you get your strength back."

This wasn't good news. "I don't have time to spare."

"You should eat something," Adrian said. "It'll help."

Dastien stood in one swift motion with me cradled in his arms. "It's dinner time anyway," he said. "Let's go. We should all eat."

He started to walk out the door, but I stopped him. "Wait. I want to say bye to Meredith."

"We'll be right behind you," Dastien said to them.

The others left as Dastien stepped up to Meredith's bed, my body still cradled in his arms.

I reached out with a shaky hand, brushing back a piece of sweaty hear from her face. Her color was worse, if that were possible. Her hand felt like skin and bones in mine. "I'm sorry. I didn't mean to pull from you, too. I only wanted to help you, but I'm making it worse." I sighed. "I talked to Donovan though. He's on his way back. We'll figure something out. Just hang on." I looked up at Dastien. "If I took power from her, can I give it back?"

"The only reason you could pull the power is because you're stronger than her. But giving it back…that's trickier."

"But I pulled from you and you're stronger than me. Aren't you?"

He shrugged. "I'm not sure who's stronger, but I'm your mate. We can send it back and forth without any cost."

"I must be really out of it, because that made a little bit of sense." I wrapped my arms around his neck. "Don't you dare give me your power."

"What do you think I'm doing right now?"

"Stop it." I didn't want him hurting like I was.

"Relax. I'm giving you a little at a time. We'll eat, and you'll be fine. We'll both be fine." He stepped into the hallway and pushed open the door to the outside with his back.

Sunlight hit my face, and my head didn't throb. I relaxed against his shoulder. "I'm feeling better already."

"Good."

"Thanks for taking care of me."

"It's my pleasure, *cherie*," he said as he started across the courtyard.

It was a different experience, trusting him as much as I did. At times it really felt like we were halves of each other. Like he was an extension of me, but also his own person. I didn't have to worry about how I acted or what I did or said. He wouldn't judge me, and he didn't mind helping me when I got in over my head.

Who would've thought that the guy I flirted with in a bookstore would one day feel like an essential part of my life?

I remembered that conversation, talking about favorite songs. It reminded me of something. "Hey, babe."

"Yeah?"

"I'm really looking forward to going dancing with you."

He rubbed his chin on the top of my head. "What made you think of that?"

"Do you remember that day in the bookstore?"

"It wasn't that long ago, *cherie*, but you could ask me again in fifty years and I'll still say yes. I'll never forget the first conversation I had with my mate."

Heat spread through my body. "That was a good day."

"It was." He paused. "You're feeling awfully

sentimental right now." It was a statement not a question.

"Yeah. Seeing what happened between Meredith and Donovan got to me."

"Ah." He left it at that, not pressing me for any questions and I really appreciated it.

"She deserves to be as happy as I am."

"She will be."

I hoped so. "Donovan really loves her."

"If they're mates, then that's definitely true."

"Right." I laughed. "At least he won't have to bite her."

He was quiet for a second. "I don't think it's been long enough for us to laugh about that."

I tightened my hold on him. "Come on. It is kind of funny."

He sighed. "If you say so...crazy girl."

I pressed a kiss to his neck. "I say so." As Dastien walked, I had a feeling I was going to regret being carried, but I couldn't muster the energy to say something.

1

Chapter Eight

I'd never really liked going into school cafeterias. Throughout my life, they'd been a place where I was ridiculed. These days, they weren't so bad. I'd found my place in the pack, and I had friends and a kick-ass mate. But as Dastien stepped into the crowded cafeteria, I wanted to crawl into a hole and hide.

Being carried was a horrible idea. "Put me down. Now."

He tightened his arms around me, cradling me against his chest. "No."

Everyone stopped and stared. Not just one or two or twenty people. Everyone. Every single person.

What was I supposed to do? Apologize for pulling all that power? Make a speech?

"Say something," Dastien whispered into my ear.

God. This was so not what I wanted to do. "Will you put me down?"

"No."

"Fine." This wouldn't be humiliating at all. I cleared my throat. "Hey, everyone. I'm sorry for taking without asking. Meredith's really sick, and I was trying to hold a connection to Donovan to find out how to break the curse. He's in the Andes right now, and it took a little bit from each of you to talk to him. So, thank you."

People shouted out questions.

"I wish I had answers for you, but I don't yet. All of you helped me get closer to finding out how to help Meredith. So, thanks again. And I'm sorry." I turned to Dastien. "Good enough?"

"Yes."

I wasn't sure I believed him, but he looked around the room and then started walking to where Adrian, Chris and Shannon were sitting. As we wove through the tables, conversations picked up again.

Dastien set me in a chair. "I'll be back with food."

"Thanks." Everyone else was already eating. Smells of fajitas and enchiladas made my stomach growl embarrassingly loud. Whoops. I put a hand over my stomach. "I guess I'm hungry."

Chris shook his head, and his blond hair fell into his eyes. He slid a small plate with a pile of Mexican rice and refried beans smothered with cheese on it my way. "Start with that." He handed me a fork.

I wasn't about to turn the food away. I gave Chris a nod, and started eating.

Dastien hadn't been gone long, but by the time he got back with my tray, I was nearly licking the plate.

"That was kind of intense," Adrian said.

I looked around the table, and they were all staring at me. "What?"

Dastien took the plate from me and set a tray down. It was piled high with Mexican food. My favorite. I could eat it for breakfast, lunch, and dinner every day and never get sick of it. It was like the cafeteria gods had read my mind today.

"I don't think I've ever been so hungry in my life," I said over my mountain of food.

"I can't watch this. It's so...disgusting." Shannon stood. "I'll be in Meredith's room."

"What's her problem? I swear you guys regularly eat way more than this."

"Yeah, but usually we take time to do things like breathe and chew," Adrian said with a chuckle.

The extreme hunger that I felt sometimes took some getting used to. My stomach had somehow turned into an endless cavern when I became a werewolf. On a normal day, I ate maybe five times as much as I did as a normal human. Or more. Whatever I'd done to talk to Donovan had really worn me out, but the food was helping.

"Sorry, guys. I'll try and slow down."

"Don't worry about it," Chris said as balanced his chair on its back legs. "I'm not upset. I'm kind of impressed. You're tucking it away like a pro."

Not even when I was recovering from being bitten by a vampire was I this drained or hungry. Although that was a different kind of drained. Or maybe it was the power that Dastien was feeding into me? He ate one-handed, and his free hand hadn't left my back. The steady pulse of his alpha power warmed me from the inside like a balm on my tired muscles.

"Everything okay?" Dastien asked.

"As long as you don't count grossing out our friends, then yeah, everything's fine." But I was feeling self-conscious about how much I was eating. "Merging witchcraft with what? Discuss options." I waved my fork at them. "And ignore what's going on over here." I waved the fork at myself. I started eating again, but tried to remember to breathe between bites this time.

"We were talking about that before you got here," Adrian said. "The only thing that we can come up with is combining types of witchcrafts. Assuming that, we have a few options."

I wished they only had one option, but I'd take what I could get. "Tell me."

"Basically there are incantations or spells, potions, and curses," Adrian said. "Although curses are like a subset of spells and incantations, but with a negative connotation. Assuming we rule out the whole curse category—"

"Wait. Why are we ruling those out?" It seemed like a bad idea to rule anything out at this point, but what did I know? For once, I wished my parents had moved us to Texas sooner, but there was nothing I could do about that.

"Because curses are dark," Dastien said. "They're meant to hurt, and we aren't going to do anything bad to one of our own."

I chewed slowly as I thought. "Agreed. What's the deal with the incantations and potions?"

"Well, sometimes they go hand-in-hand," Adrian said. "Like what your cousins gave us to fight the vampires."

They'd given us a bunch of little vials of herby-looking stuff. All I had to do was say the right phrase and chuck one at a vampire. As soon as the glass broke, the potion exploded. They were a pretty neat and had saved our butts. We wouldn't have made it out alive without the magical assistance.

"Okay, and what happens when it's just an incantation," I said.

"Sometimes all a witch—" Chris stopped when Adrian cleared his throat. "Fine. Sometimes all a *bruja* needs to do is say something. Their magic plus their will makes the words true."

"And potions are mixtures of magical ingredients that pack a punch," Adrian said. "They can do any number of things—from make someone fall in love to transform a person from human to mouse—depending on what you mix in them."

I took a break from eating. "So we need something like what I used in the cave. We should find something that mixes a potion and words to set the spell. And it should be one that makes her wolf hit the hay."

There were some grumbles around the table.
"If you guys have a better idea that won't kill her, then I'm all ears. But remember that we're only suppressing her wolf to keep her alive until we come up with something better."

"That seems really unnatural," Dastien said.

"I know." I took another bite.

"Are you sure you're not trying this because of your own issues with changing?" Chris asked

I dropped my fork with a clatter. "No. I'm not." At least I didn't think I was.

We sat in silence for a bit, each of us eating and letting the cafeteria sounds fill the void.

After a bit, Adrian spoke up. "Can I see your *Book of Shadows?*"

Shit. I'd left my bag in Meredith's room. "You didn't happen to grab my bag, did you?"

Dastien shook his head. "Sorry. It'll be fine there. No one's going to mess with your stuff."

Those books meant something to my cousins, and they meant something to me. Leaving them laying around felt wrong. "Okay," I said, shaking it off. "I'll grab them after."

"I think there was something in your family's *Book of Shadows* that could work," Adrian said. "They weren't specifically for werewolves but they talked about suppressing inner demons."

Chris cussed up a storm.

"I know. I know," Adrian said. "But to *La Alquelarre*, our inner wolf could count as a demon." He paused to let that sink in. He had a point, and I was more than a little ashamed that I looked at my wolf as a kind of demon. It made me feel out of control, which was not a fun feeling. It made me angry and violent. Two things I'd never considered myself before.

"There are still a bunch of ingredients that we don't have in storage. I'm not sure where we'd find them," Adrian said.

"I could maybe ask my mom. Even if she didn't really participate in *La Alquelarre*, my grandmother did. She might know where to find stuff." I pushed the tray to the center of the table. "I think I'm done. I'm grossing myself out now."

"Eating's part of being a Were," Dastien said. "Don't feel bad about it. I ate way more than you did."

I glanced over at his tray. He'd cleaned all of his plates. Three big dishes and two small ones.

"This tray was mine too." He pointed to another tray full of empty plates.

"Holy shit, babe." My cheeks heated. I didn't want to make them feel bad or anything, and I liked food as much as the next person, but this was insane. "It's weird, you know? Where does it go?"

"Quick digestion?" Chris said.

I rolled my eyes. "Whatever. Let's go get the books and figure out a game plan and then I'll call my mom."

Adrian nodded. "If we could get everything together by tonight, then we can do a midnight casting. It's almost the full moon. Could give us an advantage."

Sounded legit to me. "Cool. Let's do this."

Chapter Nine

When we got to the infirmary, Shannon and two girls that I didn't know were in Meredith's room. They were lost in discussion as they pawed their way through my books. One of them was pouring over the textbook, while Shannon had my family's *Book of Shadows* and the other girl had the blue book.

So much for no one messing with my stuff. I shot Dastien a look before turning my anger on them. "You went through my bag and grabbed my personal property?" I practically growled.

They jumped, and dropped the books, keeping their gazes on the ground. Except for Shannon.

She held onto the book and slowly closed it. She wasn't strong enough to meet my gaze directly, but she stared at my forehead. "We were working on helping Meredith. What you're planning is wrong. I can't let you try to suppress her wolf when she wants out."

I tried to push the wolf down, but fur rippled along my forearms. My control today was total shit. "I'm trying to *help* her, not *kill* her. Anything else we try will end in a funeral. And I don't think I gave any of you permission to dig around in my bag."

"They were given to a pack member. They're the pack's books now," Shannon said.

Was she trying to piss me off?

"Man, that was a dumb thing to say," Adrian said.

Chris grunted as the cold fury beat inside me. The fur spread, but I wasn't ready to change. I couldn't—wouldn't—let myself change.

Dastien cleared his throat. "You want to think very carefully about what you say next, Shannon."

I took the fallen books from the ground and grabbed the *Book of Shadows* out of Shannon's hand. "You two will leave here now and never speak of these books again." I let my alpha power roll out as I said the words to the two girls.

"Yes, ma'am," they said, but they were frozen in place.

"Go. Now."

Dastien held my hand, and I barely hung on to my human form.

Once they were gone, I turned to Shannon. "What the hell is your problem? I know we don't get along, but we're after the same thing."

"No. We're not." She met my gaze for a split second before looking down. "I know you've gotten close with Meredith, but I've been friends with her for years. We spent our summers together. I know what this has done to her, and I know that if there was a time to try and fix it, it's now."

"And you're willing to take that risk?"

"Yes."

I looked down at Meredith's pale form. She was drugged, and couldn't speak for herself. Maybe my reasoning was off. Everyone else thought so.

I couldn't afford to screw this up. "Guys? I'm a little out of my element here. If I'm wrong, then I'm wrong. So, let's vote."

"A pack isn't run by vote, *cherie*," Dastien said.

"Well, this isn't a pack. This is us being Meredith's friends." I turned to Adrian. "What do you think?"

He looked around the room and then crossed his arms. "Given what we know, I'm with you. Safest option is best."

"Chris?"

He ran his hands through his hair, making his blond waves stand on end. "I hate this. I really hate this."

I knew the feeling. There was no doubt that this whole situation was messed up.

"If we're going on what we know right now, I think there aren't any good options," Chris said.

Shannon growled in the corner but didn't speak up.

"But for the record," Chris continued. "I want to be on Shannon's side. I want to find another way besides making a bad situation worse. I just don't know that there is one."

I nodded. "Agreed." The guys were with me, even if they didn't want to be. "Dastien?"

"I agree. It would be good to find a way to get around this, but for now if you can help her in any way, then that would be good."

"You're not helping her," Shannon yelled. "You're making her worse. I'll not be a part of it." She slammed the door so hard the door splintered around the knob.

The room was quiet for a second.

"Well, that was super fun," I said. I rolled my shoulders back, trying to ease the tension. "Am I doing the right thing?"

"I think so. Breaking the curse is dangerous. Calming

the wolf has worked for years," Dastien said. "Her parents and three of her brothers won't get here until tomorrow, but her oldest brother is close. His flight should land in a few hours. We'll talk it out with him when he gets here. They can try to calm her wolf, too, but I don't think it's going to work." He made a face. "None of them are stronger than me."

I glanced down at Meredith. I'd met her brother in the vision. Although the word 'met' might've been a stretch. "Yeah. I'd feel better if we got the okay from her family before we did anything to her."

"We should still get the potion ready," Adrian said. "If they agree, then we'll be good to go. And if not…it'll keep us busy while we wait."

"Yeah. Let's go," Chris said as he gingerly opened the broken door.

We left the infirmary and walked to the next building over. Classes had all let out by now. Everyone else on campus was eating, studying, or working out.

The metaphysics lab was at the end of the hall. That way, if someone accidentally blew something up, not as many classrooms would be destroyed. When my lab partner told me that during my second week, I was shocked. What about the students in the classrooms? He told me in a you-gotta-be-kidding-me voice that we were werewolves. Healing wasn't a problem.

Still, I hoped we didn't blow anything up with our attempts at potion making. Healing fast didn't mean we couldn't feel pain.

Adrian opened the door and turned on the lights. The fluorescents flickered a few times before burning at full strength.

Heavy-duty metal tables took up the room, each one

with two stools. It looked like a chemistry classroom from a normal school, complete with beakers and Bunsen burners on every table. The only difference was what actually went into the beakers.

"Can I see the book?" Adrian asked as he sat at one of the tables.

I opened up my bag and pulled the little brown book out. "Be careful with it," I said as I handed it over.

"Of course."

Dastien grabbed the stools from the table behind us. We sat as Adrian placed the book gently on the table. It still had little yellow pieces of paper sticking out from it marking pages.

"We have three options, but only one really viable spell. At least that's my opinion." He opened to the first one. "This is a basic healing spell." He tapped the page and turned it so that I could read it. Little scribblings filled the margins. It called for dried sage, holy water, and an egg.

An egg? *Brujas* were weird.

I skimmed the description. It was a spell. There were steps to be performed and words to be said, but nothing that required any pre-mixing in the meta lab. As far as things went, this one seemed much easier than I'd thought it'd be. Anyone could do this.

It was too easy. "She doesn't need to be healed. She needs the wolf to chill out so that she's not fighting against the curse. And this spell doesn't mix any kinds of magic." Donovan hadn't given me much, but I was going to trust what I did have. "That option's out. Right?"

"Yeah. That's what I thought, too." He flipped to the fourth piece of yellow paper. "This one is the most complicated of the bunch."

"Dude. It says eye of newt," Chris said.

"Seriously?" I looked closer. "I didn't know that was an actual thing."

"This one would be awesome, but it calls for the blood of the caster," Adrian said.

I ran my finger down the ingredients. Sure enough, there it was. Three drops needed. Short of going back onto the compound, holding Luciana down, and taking her blood, I didn't see how I could possibly get that. "Yeah. We went over this one already. Not going to happen. Unless you're saying that there's a way around it."

Adrian shook his head. "No. But I want there to be. The potion uses the blood to break the hold the curse has on the afflicted."

I stood and paced the room as I tried to think of a way I could convince Luciana to give us some of her blood. I could bargain for it. She wanted something from me. I wanted something from her. There had to be a way for us to work it out. I pulled my hair down from its messy bun and ran my fingers through the tangles before putting it up again.

I turned back to the guys. "Maybe I can make a deal with—"

"No. Just no." Chris turned to Dastien. "You can't let her go back there. The vibe there wasn't even close to cool."

"I tried to tell her not to go earlier, and she went anyway," Dastien said. "But, for what it's worth, *cherie*, you shouldn't trust someone who would bargain with you over the life of someone else."

I chewed on my lip for a second as I thought. "You're right." I went back to the stool. "We're desperate, but not that desperate. Not yet." I leaned forward on the table. The cold metal was a shock to my warm skin. But the fact that I got zero visions because I wasn't trying to have them was another shock. I had control. I had *bruja* powers and alpha ones. I could do this. "And the last one?"

"It's our best shot," Adrian said.

"Show me," I said.

He picked the book off the table, and flipped to the right page. With a deep breath, he placed it down in front of me. "This is the one that talks about calming the inner demon. It doesn't have as many crazy, hard to get ingredients that the other one does—although there are a few in there that I have no idea what they are and some that I have no idea where we'd get them. Aside from that, it's trickier. There are more steps. Everything has to be timed. And there are three different potions involved." He paused. "Now that I'm thinking back on what you said, this is a combo of spell and potion. It could be what Donovan was talking about, but we have no real way of knowing."

I couldn't risk pulling that much power again. He'd be here tomorrow afternoon. Maybe morning if he ran really fast, but Meredith didn't have that long.

I turned to Dastien. "Can we wait for Donovan?"

"I've never seen anyone last without the wolf for so long. And I've never seen someone fade so fast. If Meredith makes it to midnight, I'll be surprised."

In other words, no. Shit. My eyes burned and I rubbed them. I couldn't cry. Not yet. We still had time. "Everything's a risk."

"There's one more thing," Adrian said.

What now? "And…"

"It has to be done exactly at midnight under the moon."

God. That seemed too soon. "How much time does that give us to get everything ready?"

Chris checked his cell phone. "It's almost five. So we'd need to have everything prepped and good to go in six hours."

"Is that enough time?"

"We'll make it enough," Adrian said.

"Okay." The pressure of what we were going to do weighed down on me. My chest constricted and I swallowed, trying to keep everything under control. "Let's do this. Right now, it's our best option. We'll get started, and when Meredith's brother gets here, we'll give him the final call."

"How are you doing?" Dastien said as he looked down at me.

"Fine."

"Your wolf. She's restless. Any chance you'll let her out?" He nudged me.

Was he nuts? "Now? You want to talk about this now?"

"Did you read the spell?"

"Yes."

"It says the person performing it has to be at one with themself."

"Yeah, I saw that."

"You're not at one with yourself, *cherie*." He pulled me toward him. "Why are you still so afraid of it?"

"I don't fucking know!" I snapped at him and instantly felt bad about it. My temper was out of control today, but Dastien didn't seem bothered by it.

"You're a beautiful chocolate brown wolf. I'd like to see that again sometime, but you've been putting it off for weeks."

When I was going through the transition from human to Were, I'd been a wolf. At one point, I kept going back and forth between forms so much that they were worried whether I'd survive. I didn't remember, but apparently the only thing keeping me together had been Dastien staying by my side.

I rocked from foot to foot. "It's weird."

Adrian and Chris laughed, but Dastien shot them a look. They shut up immediately.

"I'm going to do it. I really am…not today, though." I gave him the best smile I could. "I've gotta take care of Meredith first."

He pressed his lips in a firm line before speaking.

"You're going to have to deal with this before the full moon. Three days, Tessa. It'll give us the edge we need to fight during the Tribunal."

"I know." I got it, but I couldn't deal with it now.

"It'll be really fun. Going on a run. Feeling the wind against your face. You're going to love it. Trust me."

I trusted him, but still, letting go of my humanity was harder than expected. Doing it a little bit at a time was easier. I'd gotten much more comfortable with the pack and being Dastien's mate, and those powers were pretty cool. Being on four legs was what freaked me out.

"Meredith first, then wolfy stuff."

"Promise?"

I hated to promise if I wasn't going to follow through. Still, I kind of had to with this one so I might as well give him my word. "I promise."

"Good." He placed a quick peck against my lips.
"Now, let's raid the supply closet."

Chapter Ten

The meta lab storage room was across the hall. It was tiny, three feet by six feet at most. The door bumped precariously into the shelves that lined every inch of wall as we opened it. Every item in the room was perfectly labeled with white tape in two-inch round glass jars and alphabetically organized. The space was perfectly used. I may have been slightly jealous of the skills it took to organize at this level.

Dastien opened the door and then his cell phone rang. He pulled it from the back pocket of his jeans and glanced at the screen. "Excuse me for a sec." He stepped into the classroom next-door.

For a moment I wondered what the phone call could be about, but soon I forgot all about it. Taking one final look around the room, I turned to Adrian and Chris. "Let's get what we need from here, and figure out what we don't have. After that, I'll call my mom and see if she might know where to get the rest."

Adrian handed me the book. "Sounds like a plan. If you read, we'll pull."

"Cool." I grabbed the book. The paper was yellow and the edges were worn, but the handwriting was still readable. In the margins, someone had written, "Shortcuts result in ineffective potions." Great. So, no shortcuts. "Cinnamon."

Adrian searched, and handed the bottle to Chris.

"Next," Adrian said.

"Salt."

More muttering from the closet.

"Next."

"Flour." Wait a second. "Cinnamon? Salt? Flour? Really? What are we making? A pie?" This was supposed to be a potion, not a home economics project. "If the next thing on the list is pumpkin, I'm going to freak out."

Adrian laughed. "Cinnamon can be used as cleanser for the blood. Salt grounds any evil spirits. Flour—"

"Did someone say we needed pumpkin?" Chris stepped out of the room with a can of pumpkin puree.

"Jesus Christ. I think my cousins made a mistake and gave me the family cookbook." I closed the little brown book. "They could at least call it something better than cinnamon. Like bark from the center ring of an ancient tree." I wiped sweat from my forehead. My wolf was rising along with my nerves. "If we mix these things up, I'm pretty sure we're gonna make some really bad cookies."

Adrian grinned. "These are just the ingredients. It's what you do with them that makes them either cookies or a potion. Give it a chance to work."

The thought that we could be doing the wrong thing made my mouth dry. I was so out of my element, but I was trying to go along with it. Still, this whole thing seemed really far-fetched.

I chewed on my lip, trying to find my calm but failing

miserably. I hadn't thought about what went into a potion. "How about we skip to the hard stuff? I'll let you gather all this nonsense."

"Actually, that's not a bad idea. Might take longer to get all the other stuff together," Adrian said. "Give me the book, and I'll make a list."

Dastien swung open the classroom door. His wavy hair was disheveled, like he'd been messing with it while he was on the phone. A pulse of anxiety flowed through our bond, and for once, it wasn't mine.

"Everything okay?"

"Tribunal stuff."

Yikes. Not something I wanted to deal with tonight, but I hated to see him upset. "Everything okay?"

"We'll see. What's going on?" Dastien asked, changing the subject.

I considered pushing him to find out what the phone call had been about, but decided against it. If he didn't want to talk about it, I wouldn't force him. "Adrian's making a list. You want to go with me to find this stuff?"

"Sure, where're we going?"

"No idea."

My phone rang in my bag, Aphex Twin's 'Polynomial-C' telling me that it was Axel. I ran back through the lab, and answered it. "Hey, bro."

"You rang?"

"Yeah. Like forever ago."

"Sorry. I kind of had a night, so I slept in and then had classes."

I laughed. "No shit. I got the email."

"Jesus. I don't remember emailing you. What'd it say?"

"Hilarious stuff. You'll never live this one down." I grinned as I remembered his confession about a girl he was crushing on. "But hey, I might need your help."

"What'd you do now?"

"Why does it have to be something that I did?" I said as I walked to the window of the lab.

"Come on. I'm your brother."

I blew out a breath, fogging up the glass. "Well, it's not me. It's Meredith. I don't know if I told you, but she's been cursed by Luciana."

The sharp exhale on the other end of the line told me he knew all about Luciana.

I walked back across the room. "Meredith was fine, but that changed this morning. I need help finding some ingredients. Any chance you'd know of a place to get things like—" Adrian handed me a piece of paper. I glanced down at it. "Hundred year old sainted ashes?" I looked up at Adrian and he shrugged. Right. A saint's ashes to get rid of a demon. Made sense. But who in the hell kept ashes of a saint around the house?

"I might know of a place, but I'd have to go with you."

Whoa. Seriously? I thought it might be a long shot at best, but he must've been keeping up with the coven more than I'd thought while he was at school in Austin. "That's fine. It'd be good to see you. I missed you on Sunday." The only time I really went off St. Ailbe's grounds was for Sunday lunches at my parents' house. Dastien always went with me, and some of the others, too, to make sure I didn't lose control. But last Sunday, Axel hadn't made it back from college.

"Aww, sis. That's so sweet." His voice had a whining-tease to it.

"Shut up. I hate you." But we both knew that was a total lie.

He laughed. "Meet me outside my dorm?"

"Sure. I'll leave now, but it'll still take me a bit to get there." We were a good hour-and-a-half away, and that was if there was no traffic at all.

"Cool. Text me when you get here."

"Will do. Later." I put my phone away. The guys were staring at me.

"Really? You think he knows a place?" Adrian asked.

I shrugged. "He said so." He was my brother. I trusted him with my life. And Meredith's. "You two get to working on this stuff, and Dastien and I will cover the rest. We cool?"

"Yup. Go. We got this," Chris said.

I looked up at Dastien. "How about you? Is it okay if you leave campus all day?"

He raised an eyebrow. "Yeah. I think it's fine."

"That wasn't what I meant. Aren't you supposed to be teaching? And keeping the animals under control?"

He grinned. "Yes, to both. But they'll be okay for a couple hours and I called one of my Cazador friends to fill in for my martial arts classes. It's fine. Let's go." He started to walk out. "But I'm driving."

"What? No, I'll drive."

"Not a chance."

I followed him into the hallway, waving at Chris and Adrian over my shoulder. "Later, guys."

***

Dastien ended up driving, but that was fine because that meant I got control of the radio. We chatted and listened to music the whole drive to Austin. Finding something to talk about with him was never hard. Neither was being quiet. It was comfortable. Even when I felt like I was going crazy, being around Dastien made me feel calm.

He'd said it was because he was a strong alpha, and that centered my wolf. I wasn't so sure that was it. I'd like to think that if neither of us were werewolves, if we were normal humans, that it would be just as easy. I'd feel just as comfortable.

"What?" He asked as he pulled off the highway.

"Nothing."

"It's not nothing. What are you thinking? I want to know."

"You don't have to know everything I think."

"No. But I can tell you're happy, and if I did something that made you feel that way, I'd like to know so I can make you feel that way again."

I leaned against the window so that I could get a better view of him. "You didn't have to do anything. You were you, and that's more than enough."

"*Cherie.*" His voice was low and gravelly as he glanced at me. That voice did things to me.

It wasn't long before we reached UT's campus. Axel's dorm wasn't far off the main drag. It was a massive two-building dorm. To me it looked a little dreary. All that brick with these teeny-tiny windows and closet-sized rooms with beds that pulled out from the walls, but Axel said he didn't mind. He liked being with all the people.

I texted him that we were parked on the street in front of his dorm, and he walked up a second later. No one would ever doubt that we were siblings. He wasn't as short as me, but we had similar features—wavy dark brown hair, dark brown eyes, light skin. His nose was a little bigger than mine, but the same shape. And our eyes were exactly the same.

"Hey, sis. Dastien," he said as he jumped in.

"How you feeling?"

"Like shit, but it's my own damned fault. Would be nice to have some of those werewolf healing abilities."

Dastien laughed as he pulled away from the curb. "Then you wouldn't have been able to get drunk in the first place."

"No shit?"

"Nope. Metabolism burns off the alcohol quicker than you can drink."

"Seriously?" Axel hummed as he thought. "What if you drank straight Everclear?"

Dastien shook his head. "Still wouldn't get you drunk."

These guys were ridiculous. "Not to interrupt, but where are we going?"

"Right. We're going north on I-35. You're going to meet our Great-Aunt Rosa."

I twisted in my seat. "We have a Great-Aunt Rosa?"

Axel's eyes were wide. "I know, right? Who knew?"

I faced front again. "Would've been nice if Mom hadn't kept me so in the dark." Being ignorant was seriously frustrating. "What's Rosa's deal? Why doesn't she live with *La Aquelarre*?"

"They had a falling out after *abuela* died. Luciana was the problem. That's why Claudia and Raphael's parents aren't around much. They technically live there, but spend most of the time traveling to avoid Luciana."

"Why didn't they move away?"

"Because the twins didn't want to. They were still learning and needed to be around the rest of the coven to do that. Now that they know more, they want to stick around to support whoever inherits the position from Lucicana."

I scoffed at that. "Sounds like shit parenting to me.

Who abandons their kids to an evil witch? No wonder mom isn't close with her sister anymore."

Axel directed us into a neighborhood of cute, brightly colored houses. We stopped in front of one with a beautiful garden in front. Wildflowers lined the walkway to the front door, giving it a laid back feel instead of a manicured look like its neighbors.

As we stepped up to the front stoop, the door swung open. A short, round, white-haired woman stood in the doorway. Her skin was paper-thin and wrinkled, and her shoulders hunched over, making me feel tall—quite an accomplishment for someone who was barely over five feet. She was in a flower printed dress, and a pair of reading glasses with bright red frames hung from her neck on a beaded chain.

"I wondered when you might come," she said. Her voice was a little nasal and reedy, but pleasant.

"Me?" I pointed to myself.

"Yes. You." She moved aside. "Come." She motioned to the floor. "But watch the salt."

A line of salt covered the threshold. The line continued across the porch and around the corners on both sides, sealing the house in a circle. For protection?

From who? Luciana?

Stepping over the salt, I walked into the house. The floorboards creaked under my weight. The place smelled old and musty, but there was a warmth to the space. The incense that burned somewhere in the house blotted out most of the musk, leaving it smelling like a church.

I sneezed. And sneezed. And again. I pulled my shirt over my face, but I couldn't stop.

"Tess?" Dastien said. I felt his hand on my arm, but I couldn't stop sneezing.

"That's what I thought. Lead her into the living room," Rosa said.

I couldn't see. I was sneezing so fast my eyes were glued shut. I could barely get enough air to breathe. I knew I was breathing—sneezing took air—but this was out of control.

I reached out blindly, until I grasped Dastien.

"Out." Sneeze. "Now." Sneeze. "Now." Leaving this house was the only answer. It was the incense. I had to go. Right then.

Dastien lifted me, but Rosa started speaking in rapid Spanish. I was sneezing so much, I couldn't focus on the words, but Dastien understood her. He said something and then put me back down on the couch. "She's going to help."

"Incense." Sneeze. "Out."

"It's not the incense, *cherie*. Luciana cursed you when you went onto the coven's land. Which was why I didn't want you to go in the first place." The last bit was very growly.

Shit. This wasn't good. I kept sneezing. My abs were getting a hell of a workout.

Something slimy rubbed under my nose and the smell of eucalyptus and mint filled my senses. The sneezing slowed. I could finally open my eyes in between the wracking breaths.

The walls of the house were covered with religious icons. The aged paintings of saints' faces stared down at me. There wasn't a bit of empty space anywhere. Even the curtains had writing on them, and I'd bet everything I had that the words were Bible verses.

If I weren't related to Rosa, I'd say this was the home of a crazy person. After all, I didn't really know the lady. She probably was insane.

She stood in front of me, close enough that I could smell the rose and faint garlic on her skin above everything else. She held a white egg in one hand as she leaned over me. The shell was ice cold as she rubbed it over my head. She ran it in a circular motion down my body from head to foot as she said the Lord's Prayer in Spanish. As she moved the egg, the sneezing trickled to a stop.

What the hell was going on?

When she was done, she reached for a glass on the coffee table. We were all silent as we waited for something to happen, but I wasn't sure what.

The sound of Rosa cracking the egg against the edge of the glass startled me. She dumped the innards into the glass, but something was wrong with it. The yolk was black and the white had turned a cloudy gray.

"Holy shit," Axel said.

"Watch your language," Rosa said.

I sat up, swinging my legs over the edge of the couch to get a closer look. "What the hell is that?"

"You, too." She held the glass up to the light so I could get a good look at it before handing it to me. "*That* is a curse."

"What!" I nearly dropped it.

Rosa took the cup from my shaking hand. "Did Luciana touch you while you were there?"

I thought back, replaying the scene in my mind. "No."

"Did she say anything odd? Make any motions with her hands?"

I was suddenly cold. "Yes. Yes, she did. She said something, but I couldn't make it out and she waved her hand. It felt like she slapped me, but there was no way for her to have physically done that. She couldn't actually have reached me."

"And how did you feel after?"

How had I felt? I'd nearly changed. My wolf tried to claw its way out. But I'd been pissed. It was normal to be easily angered, especially around the full moon. Right? "I...my wolf was upset." Oh shit. She'd wanted me to feel out of control. Luciana had made the point to tell me she could make me feel better, but when I hadn't agreed, she'd made sure I'd start feeling worse. She was banking on the fact that if I lost control of my wolf, then maybe I'd go to her.

She was trying to trap me.

"I thought it was normal to feel on edge so close to the full moon," I said to Dastien.

"To an extent, but you've been on the verge of shifting all day. The only time you weren't was when you were recovering your power after dealing with Meredith."

I looked back at Rosa. "I thought breaking a curse was hard. Dangerous."

"I'm old enough to know what's dangerous. This," she held out the nasty black-egg-filled glass again, "is an easy one to break. Child's play. No real harm done, and it would've worn off in a day on its own. I only sped things up."

That made me feel only moderately better.

"So, *mijita*, what can I do for you?"

I pulled the list out of my back pocket. "I'm trying to make a potion, and it calls for these." I handed her the paper.

She pulled on her glasses. When she was done reading, she met my gaze. "This is quite a list."

"Yes."

"And what are you going to do with these things?"

I explained about Meredith and the curse. About how sick she was. And finally our plan to help her.

When I was done, Rosa sat down next to me. "I'm going to help you, but I want you to know that this is dangerous. All magic is to some extent, but what Luciana does...it's dark. Black." She leaned back. "I couldn't stay around so much blackness without risking my soul."

I wasn't sure what to say to that. "Is it really that bad?"

"Not always. You must understand that your intent matters so much more than the words in the spell. The words may be gibberish or a beautiful poem, but it's what you intend to do with those words that matters. A little bit of your heart goes into each work you do. If you're a dark person, like Luciana, you do dark things. If you're light, you do light things. And when you're a part of a coven, a little bit of what is done there rubs off on each person."

Chills ran down my arms. I was suddenly so glad Mom kept me away all those years.

Rosa patted my cheek as she gazed into my soul. "You will do light things."

The only thing I could do was nod. I was completely mesmerized by her gaze.

"Good." She held up the list. "I will get you these ingredients, but with them you must do only light. Only light." She poked my sternum. "You put a light heart in with the potion and words. You put your love into what you say and the magic will not harm you. But if you stray into the dark in your thoughts with these ingredients...the magic will be tainted and it will darken your soul. You must think only of the light."

I nodded. "I will."

Rosa's knees cracked as she stood back up, and Dastien gave her a hand. "Thank you, honey." She patted his cheek and slowly waddled into the next room.

"What's on the list?" Axel whispered.

"Saints' ashes, oil from a weeping icon, feathers and blood from a black chicken...you know, the usual," I said.

Axel laughed. "Nice."

Rosa held a brown paper bag when she came back. She rolled the top of it down a few times before handing it to me. "One more thing, before you go." She looked at my feet. "Shoes off."

I wasn't one to obey a command, and I didn't think twice about it. I pulled off my socks and shoes.

She had a tiny vial of liquid. Dipping in a Q-tip, she moved toward me. She traced a cross over the center of my forehead as she said a prayer. She did the same to my cheeks and chin before motioning for me to hold out my hands. She dipped the Q-tip back into the liquid, and did the same to the tops of my hands, then palms.

"Feet."

I lifted them into the air, and she did the same to the tops of my feet.

She finished by putting her hand on the top of my head and saying a final prayer. Her words were soft and so fast that I couldn't make them out. The little bits and pieces I could hear were sort of Catholic, but different.

The top of my head grew hot as she prayed, and by the time she finished, I felt much lighter—as if a weight had been lifted. It might've sounded crazy to say that I was touched by a higher power, but that's what it felt like.

"There. I've given you a blessing. I hope it keeps you safe. I'm going to light some *lámparas* for you tonight."

"Thanks." I cleared my throat. "I thought witchcraft and Christianity were separate."

She laughed as she capped the little bottle. "Oh, they

can be. Very much so. But when the Catholics came to this land they combined their religion with our old ways. In Peru, you'll see the Virgin as the Pacha Mama. It might not seem very Catholic, but it made for an easy blending of our peoples."

She grinned, and if possible, the wrinkles around her eyes deepened. "Spirituality is very personal. And what a person pulls from their magic, that's personal, too. It's why I said the words don't matter so much. I use my faith in God to back the little things I can do. It helps me to use His words. Others find their faith and will in other things. Does that make sense?"

I thought for a second. It kind of really did. "Yes. I think so." And I liked it. Mom had always raised us going to church. I liked that if I did do this whole *bruja* thing, I didn't have to give up my childhood beliefs. I'd already given up enough of my old life.

I put my socks and shoes back on. "Thank you for everything."

"*De nada, mijita.* If Luciana gives you trouble again, you come back. Don't try to fight what you don't yet understand."

I nodded. "I think I'll do that."

She opened up her arms, and I hugged her. "Follow your heart. It's good." She pulled back. "And keep that one around." She winked at Dastien. "He's nice to look at, no?"

I laughed at the uncomfortable look on Dastien's face. "He sure is."

Axel hugged Rosa. "Thank you."

"Come back this weekend, *mijito.* I've something to show you. And you can tell me how your sister does."

"Sure thing, *Tía.*" He kissed her cheek.

126

Chapter Eleven

We dropped Axel back at his dorm, and sped back to campus. I felt lighter. Like I knew what I was doing, and everything seemed a little more in control. That lightness that Rosa talked about was nearly tangible.

Traffic was thick, so it took us forever to get back. Dastien tried to keep my mind off of everything, switching music, talking about DJs coming to town, but with each passing moment, the bag of ingredients weighed heavier in my lap. I needed to focus on what I was going to do tonight.

By the time we finally pulled through St. Ailbe's gates, I'd convinced myself that I could do this. The ingredients were all here. Everything was lining up, and even if it wasn't easy, I hadn't hit that many road bumps.

Okay, so the curse was not cool at all, but I was going to let that one go. Focusing on Meredith was key, and I'd gotten everything I needed for the spell.

Even counting the curse, everything still seemed a little easy. I wasn't sure if that was a good sign or not. Usually, it meant that the proverbial shit was about to hit the fan, but maybe I was finally on the right path and this was how things were meant to go.

Dastien left to go check on something, but I wasn't paying much attention. I waved him off and jogged to the metaphysics classroom. As soon as I stepped into the stairwell, I could smell the stench coming from the labs. It was horrendous. I shoved my nose under my T-shirt, but it didn't help. The closer I got, the worse it smelled.

I plugged my nose and opened the door. "What are you two yahoos up to?"

They were huddled over some beakers on a table by the window. When they turned to look at me, I laughed. They had clothespins on their noses.

"Do a girl a favor and toss one my way. This stuff is rank." I caught the pin that Chris tossed, and quickly clamped my nose. It hurt like a bitch, but it was better than the stench. Now I could actually walk into the classroom.

Two cookie sheets rested on a lab table covered in what looked like a solid layer of hard candy on them. A mixture was boiling in a beaker over a Bunsen burner.

I started to say something but Adrian held up a finger.

As I watched, the mixture in the beaker turned from a bubbling brownish-yellow sludge to bright blue. Chris grabbed it off of the fire with a pair of tongs and placed it in an ice bath. I leaned down to look at the little balls of black floating in the blue. The urge to touch it was strong, but I ignored it.

"What is that?" My voice sounded funny with the clothespin on my nose.

"That's the part of the second potion." Adrian pointed to one of the cookie trays. "We've got to pulverize that into a fine powder for the first component, and it's got a couple more steps." He pointed to the other cookie sheet with white and gray speckled stuff on it. "That's the third. We still have one more step for that one."

"Okay. What can I do to help?"

"You got the rest?" Chris said.

I held out my booty. "I sure do."

"Nice work. Let's see it."

I emptied the contents of the bag onto the lab table.

One small jar of ashes.

Two black feathers.

A small bottle of brownish congealed liquid. Blood. Yuck.

A thimble-sized bottle with a cotton ball soaked in a light yellow oil.

Adrian picked up the last bottle. "Whoa. I can't believe you found all this stuff."

"Honestly, me neither. But apparently I have a great aunt Rosa who has everything."

"Sweet. I need this for the blue potion," Chris said, picking up the tiny bottle of oily cotton balls. "Where's Dastien?"

"Checking on stuff." I motioned to the potions. "So, what now?"

"We saved some steps for you to do. Since you're the one who has to cast the spell, your energy has to go into it." Adrian handed me some papers and a hammer.

I glanced down at the papers. They were photocopies of the spell book. When I looked up at him sharply, he said, "Just for now. We can destroy them after if you want. But we each needed to know what the steps are."

That was reasonable. "Fine."

"Okay, so we're here." He pointed at the sheet. "The next step is to break that one up," he pointed to the brownish-yellow stuff on the cookie sheet. "When it's in smaller pieces, you can use the mortar and pestle to grind it." He pointed to the large black stone on the table. "It's a pain, but you have more control over the powder with it, and if we use a blender, the friction causes heat which would mess the whole thing up. Once that's done, we add the blood and minced feather."

"Gross." I took the cookie sheet to the next table over and started pounding at the sheet of solid potion. Whatever it was, the stuff was as hard as granite. A few more whacks and a jagged crack formed. After that, a couple more whacks and it shattered into manageable chunks. I read through the steps in the spell. It needed to be as fine as powdered sugar.

This was going to take a while.

Working in circular motion to break the pieces faster, I separated out sections in the mortar and did a little at a time. It was boring as hell, but we had to get this right.

By the time the consistency was powdered sugar-like, I was sweating. I found a knife in the supply closet, and started mincing the feathers. The spell said that they had to be finely diced, but not grain-like. I got to chopping. I rocked the knife back and forth on the table and found the motion to be surprisingly soothing. When the little bits seemed small enough, I added them in.

The book said it needed three stirs, counter-clockwise.

That done, I moved onto the next step. The blood.

I stared at the jar. I didn't like it. Not one bit.

I carefully unscrewed the lid and looked down at the paper again. "Christ. We need an eighth of a cup of this stuff?"

Chris paused from the green thing that he was breaking up to check his copy. "Yup. You got something to measure it?"

"Yeah." I took a breath and focused on happy thoughts, even if the blood made me a little queasy. I carefully measured it—not wanting to spill any on myself—and poured it into a glass pyrex, stirring to mix the elements together until it formed a thick paste, and then stopped stirring. Over-stirring would nullify the mixture. "This looks really foul."

"Good thing you don't have to eat it," Chris said.

I made a gagging sound and the guys cracked up.

"Cool. I'll take care of the last step on this one. I think this other step needs you to give it some of your juju."

Sounded awesome. I didn't want to be around this sludge more than I had to be.

Adrian brought over two beakers. One had little green pieces that looked like bits of dried leaves. The other was the diced up stuff that had been on the other cookie sheet—it was now tiny little bits of black and white that looked like pencil shavings. "Mix these two with the ashes." He handed me another beaker. "Put it in here, teaspoon by teaspoon. First, a spoonful of the green stuff. Then, a teaspoon of ash. After that, white and black shavings. Then, shavings, ash, green. Green, ash, shavings. Got it?"

Maybe not, but I had it on my copies. "We're at this part?" I pointed to the step.

Adrian nodded. "Exactly."

"Got it." I started the process, measuring everything out. Each time I measured and mixed, I tried to think of a happy memory with Meredith. Her teaching me moves in Martial Arts. Laughing at night before bed. Having a *Buffy* marathon in her room.

The beaker was nearly full when Dastien arrived. He wore his usual dark jeans, but his T-shirt made me laugh.

It had a large Above and Beyond Group Therapy logo across the front. I'd gotten it for him last week. "Cool shirt," I said.

He caught a nose pin that Chris threw his way. "This cute chick got it for me." He winked at me, and plugged his nose. There was nothing sexy about a guy wearing a clothes pin, but the way he walked, so confidently, without making a sound, he almost made it work. Almost, but not quite.

I turned to see what the other guys were doing. Adrian was shaving a block of what looked like white soap with a peeler into the nasty blood mixture. It looked like curls of Parmesan cheese floating in upchuck.

Chris was slowly pouring a blue gelatinous mess into a vial through a glass funnel. It was barely moving. Sloping down the funnel little bit by little bit.

"Do you want help pouring that? I could mush it—"

"No!" Adrian and Chris said.

I held up my hands. "Okay. Okay. Jeeze."

Adrian sighed. "It can't be touched by anything other than glass right now. It's really volatile."

I widened my eyes at Dastien, who shrugged. Apparently I was the third-place witch now. I'd have to make a point of catching up on the *bruja* training after all this was behind us.

"We set up the roof for the ritual while everything was baking. We're going to need Meredith there in fifteen."

Dastien nodded. "I'll get her and Dr. Gonzales."

"That's probably a good idea," Adrian said.

I shuddered. I didn't have anything against the good doctor, but her love of needles…those I had something against.

He brushed a kiss on my forehead. "Be back in a few."

I tapped my fingers on the table. Nerves were working their way back into my thoughts. "Am I forgetting something?"

"Maybe you want to read the incantation? It can't hurt to be familiar with it."

"Probably a good idea." I remembered what Rosa said, that the words themselves didn't matter, but it would be good to have the gist of it down. It was going to be my will, my faith, my heart that made this spell work or not work.

The pressure had only gotten heavier in the last few hours. I'd never done anything like this before. It wasn't anything like saying a few words and tossing vials at vampires. Meredith was my best friend.

I took the spell book from Adrian. "I'm going to make it work."

My voice didn't waiver as I spoke, and I almost believed myself.

***

The night was quiet as we walked out on the roof. Air conditioning units and their ventilation pipes stuck out in various places. I appreciated the three-foot-high ledge along the edge. Heights and me weren't exactly the best of friends. Meredith might argue differently, given that in my first two weeks at St. Ailbe's, I'd jumped out windows no less than four times. I'd walked away from each fall, but I didn't plan on making a habit of death-defying leaps.

We walked around the air conditioning units, heading to where the spell area was set up. A Meredith-sized circle was drawn in white chalk on the roof within a circle of candles. The largest candles marked north, south, east, and west, and the smaller ones made up the distance in between. A table was set to the side of the circle. We placed the three beakers on the table. A large copper pot sat on the table, too. The modern day version of a cauldron, apparently.

"Double, double, toil and trouble," I said.

"I thought it was 'Bubble, bubble, toil and trouble,'" Chris said.

"No. 'Double, double, toil and trouble. Fire burn and cauldron bubble.' Gotta get your Shakespeare learnin' on, boy."

Chris chuckled. "Nerd."

"This isn't a joke, y'all," Adrian said. "We're here to be serious. You've got to respect the process if it's going to work."

I hadn't meant to make fun of it. Or him. "I'm sorry. It's the nerves. This has to work, you know?"

Dastien and Dr. Gonzales came through the door with another tall blond guy. He was older than the version of him I'd seen in the vision. His hair was longer, past his shoulders and tied back in a low ponytail. He cradled Meredith in his arms. She looked so frail, with her head lolling to the side. Her lungs rattled with every breath. The drugs were keeping her alive, but only barely. He stepped over the chalk, and lowered Meredith into the center of the circle.

"I should've brought her a pillow or something," Chris mumbled.

"At least she's not puking anymore. With any luck, when she wakes up, this will be like a bad dream for her." Thinking positive was going to be my new thing. Light. I was going to be like the light.

Her brother stepped up to me. "I'm Max."

I shook his hand. "Tessa."

He exhaled and stared at his sister. "I hear you're going to help her."

"I'll do my best. But if you'd rather I not...I mean it's not a guarantee. It could end up hurting her more or—"

"No. I've heard about it. Your mate and I had a long talk."

Huh. That was what Dastien was up to.

"Meredith doesn't have much time left. Hours really," Max said, his voice broke.

I glanced at Dr. Gonzales and she nodded. "I'm almost out of options in terms of treatments. The sedative I've been using isn't working as well. She's already built up an immunity. I thought the injections would last longer, but we're out of time."

"And Donovan?" I asked Dastien.

He shook his head.

Great. I had never felt so afraid of anything. My best friend's life was in my hands. The responsibility of it made it hard for me to breathe. I stared at Meredith's prone form, barely more than skin and bones at this point.

"You're her best shot."

I swallowed, unable to trust my voice.

"She might be my sister, but I was fifteen when she was born. It's almost like she's my daughter, too. You know? Thank you for helping."

I cleared my throat. "Let's see what happens before throwing out any thank yous."

He nodded and went to stand to the side with Dr. Gonzales, Dastien, and Chris.

"You can do this. Stay positive," Adrian said.

I stepped closer to the circle, trying to believe his words. I had to do this. There weren't any other acceptable options.

It wasn't anything hard or complicated. The book said I had to light the candles in a specific order and say some words. I'd written them down on a piece of scratch paper, but I didn't think I'd need it. Rosa said that it wasn't the specific words that mattered, but the intent. That was something that was ingrained in my soul.

After I lit the candles, all I had to do was combine the three ingredients together in a pot, in a specific order, then light the mixture on fire. When it burned out, I had to blow the ashes over Meredith. If all went well, my spell would settle over the top of Luciana's spell and quiet the wolf again. I wasn't sure what kind of sign we'd get if it worked, but I figured at the very least her color would improve.

Adrian stepped over to the table where he'd placed the components of the potion. "We've got everything here. It should work." His gaze met mine. "This really should work."

I didn't know if he was trying to convince me or himself. The problem was that it didn't seem that hard. Lighting a few candles and dumping some stuff in a pot, and that was it? It had to be harder than this. Were we missing something?

What did I know? This wasn't exactly my area of expertise. I had no other choice but to trust the guys, the book, and myself.

If it didn't work, we'd try something else. I had no idea what, but I'd figure something out. "What time is it?"

"Two minutes to midnight."

All right. Game time. "I start with north, right?" I asked to buy myself a moment.

"Yep," Dastien said.

I let out a breath. This was going to work. "Who's got

the lighter?"

"Oh, right." Adrian searched the ground and then rushed to the side of nearest AC unit. He brought back a box of long stick matches. "Here you go."

I took a match from the box, and ran it along the rough side. The match flared to life, and I could tell from the sudden stillness around me that I wasn't the only one holding my breath.

"Hold this." I handed the box to Chris as I knelt. "Holy Archangel Michael, defend us in battle," I started saying the prayer as I pressed the match to the wick. It didn't light right away. Instead, it was as if the candle waited for me to finish saying the words before bursting into a foot tall flame.

I nearly fell back, but caught myself and moved to the next candle. With each part of the prayer said, the candles burned higher than natural. When I got to the East candle, the flames changed color, from yellow to orange, growing another foot in height. When I got to the South candle, they turned red and grew taller still.

It was getting hotter on the roof. I kept a strong grip on the match. It should've started to burn down, but the flame hadn't moved past the match head. I tried not to be freaked out. Instead, I focused on putting good energy into what I was doing. Thinking of light. Putting my love for Meredith into what I said. Following the spell instructions step-by-step, just like the book instructed. Finishing one candle, and then moving on to the next.

By the time I got to the West, sweat was rolling down my face. My hands were shaking. I pressed the match to the wick, and the flames changed to blue.

Meredith writhed and moaned on the floor. I froze. Had I done something wrong?

"Keep going," Adrian said.

Chris muttered something, but I couldn't make out the words.

I blew out a shaky breath. The need to finish the circle filled my mind. It had to be done. I moved faster than I had before. When I said the words for the last time and brought the match to the candle, the flames merged, forming a wall of flames that burned in a beautiful white light. Pure. I could barely see Meredith inside the ring of fire, but I knew in my soul that she was safe. I cupped my hand along the back of the match, and gently blew it out.

"Tess. You need to move through this part faster," Adrian said. "You're running out of time with the spell's potency."

Shit. Chris pulled me to my feet.

I stepped over to the table, and wiped my hands on my jeans. I didn't want to accidentally drop any of the potions. Meredith might not make it until tomorrow, even if we could redo all of this.

I peeked at the spell book. The nasty blood sludge was the first to go into the pot. Just a half a teaspoon. Then one tablespoon of the ash mixture and two drops of the blue liquid. I had to repeat each step three times.

"Why didn't we do this all before?" I asked.

"Because it has to be fresh. The potion doesn't last long once it's mixed."

"Right." I started the process, trying to hurry but at the same time, be meticulous about it. My hands shook as I worked. A feeling of unease moved through me, but I shoved it down. There wasn't time to question things. I double checked the book, and added the second round of ingredients.

I thought of good. I was going to help Meredith. I

pictured her happy and healthy in my mind.

When I was done, I stepped back from the table and waited.

I'd been hoping something would happen as I added everything together, like how the candles changed, but nothing did. Something was wrong. "Are you sure this spell is right?"

"Yes. Be confident. It won't work if you aren't," Adrian said, and I wanted to punch him. Without meaning to, he was undermining every bit of confidence I had.

A headache started brewing, making me feel woozy.

God. I hoped I was bringing the light or whatever the hell I was supposed to be doing.

I felt Dastien behind me before he put his hands on my shoulders. "Calm, *cherie*. You can do this."

I let out a shaky breath. "Okay. But I'm starting to think this isn't such a good idea. What if there's something wrong with the spell? Or with the ingredients? Or something."

Chris and Adrian started arguing quietly, but my ears were ringing—making it hard to hear them.

"No. It's right. We triple checked it. I promise. This is going to work. Believe in it," Adrian said.

"Okay." But I wasn't sure I meant it.

Maybe I was being crazy. Nerves were getting to me, but I was almost done. I shoved the doubts away.

This was my plan. We were adding to the curse, but it was to help Meredith. Once the wolf was quiet, she'd be fine again.

Chris handed me a match and held out the box. I ran the tip against the side, and it flared to light. I mustered all the will I could, believing my will was stronger than Luciana's, and said the words. "May God rebuke this demon, we humbly pray." I lowered the flaming match to the top of the pot. "Our Lord and Savior, please cast out the demon that holds this child. Bind her soul to you, and let her be free of all impurities. Amen." As soon as the fire touched the mixture it ignited with an explosion that knocked me on my back.

"Holy shit. It worked," Adrian said.

I scrambled up and looked into the pot. Barely a teaspoon of fine white powder lay in the bottom. I scooped up the powder into my left hand, trying to make sure I got every last little bit. Then I turned to the circle of flames and blew the ash toward Meredith.

Instead of flying out of my hands, it was as if the little white grains had minds of their own. The powder glided through the air, roiling on nonexistent winds. As it hit the circle of candles, the flames lowered. The grains settled over Meredith, and she moaned.

The candles grew taller and so bright that I had to block the heat from my face as I fell back a step.

And then, as suddenly as they'd flared to life, the candles went out. All was still. Only little, barely-there circles of wax on the roof showed they'd ever existed.

Meredith moaned loader.

"Meredith?" Adrian asked as he knelt beside her. "You feeling anything?"

She slowly sat up. "Yeah. I think I feel better."

Thank God.

Max knelt beside her. "Hey, cutie pie."

"Max?"

"Yeah. How's your wolf? How are you doing?"

"I'm okay. Actually…" She sat up, and my heart started racing. "I don't know…" She gasped. "I…I—" She rolled over onto her hands and knees and threw up.

My limbs felt numb as a trail of blood hit the roof.

"Oh fuck." I stumbled back a few steps. This couldn't be happening.

It hadn't worked. I'd failed.

I had a second to be upset before Meredith fell on her side, convulsing.

Chris and Adrian were kneeling beside her. Max reached out to restrain her. "No," Dr. Gonzales said as she searched for something in her bag. "Don't! You could hurt her."

It felt like an eternity passed as she shook.

Dr. Gonzales jabbed a shot into Meredith's arm. She waited a second, but when the convulsions didn't stop, Dr. Gonzales reached back into her bag. Another shot of meds slowed the convulsions, but they didn't stop. One more shot and Dr. Gonzales waited as Meredith's movements slowed.

Two more shots and Meredith was finally sedated again. It seemed to take forever for her twitching to stop completely as the drug worked its way through her body.

When she was finally still, the doctor picked up the discarded pile of shots with shaking hands. "I need to get more meds. I'm not sure how long this will hold her. Let's get her back to the infirmary."

Max gathered Meredith up in his arms again. No one said anything as they left.

I met Adrian's gaze. "I did something wrong. I messed up."

"No, I don't think you did."

No matter what the guys said, I had to have done something wrong. "I fucked it up. That's the only answer." I hugged myself as I shivered.

"Maybe we had it wrong from the beginning." Adrian

cursed.

"How? What did we miss?" I felt lightheaded, and swayed on my feet.

Dastien's scent hit me before he wrapped his arms around my waist. I leaned into him as I looked out over the edge of the building. The whole roof smelled like burnt candles, potion, and Meredith's blood and puke, but I didn't care. I stared out into the night, and wondered how I'd messed up so badly. I'd followed the spell exactly like it was written, but something had gone wrong.

The hardest part to swallow was that I'd hurt Meredith, and that made me ill. I shivered in the night.

"It wasn't your fault," Dastien said.

"Yes, it was. I meddled in something I know nothing about, and now Meredith is paying the price." It wasn't fair. "I should've taken the deal. I should've agreed to what Luciana wanted."

"You really trust that she'd follow through with her end of the bargain?"

If I was being honest with myself, no, but Meredith's life was on the line. Wasn't it worth the gamble?

"It's not yours to fix this problem. It never was," Dastien said. "This happened before you got here and it had nothing to do with you. You tried to help, and Meredith's still hanging on. We might think of something else…"

We were quiet for a second.

"It might not have been my problem to solve before, but it is now." My mother didn't call me stubborn for nothing. I didn't care what I had to do. This curse wasn't killing my friend. I'd never let that happen.

Chapter Twelve

Meredith's breath rattled in and out as I sat in the leather chair. I watched her sleep, trying to figure out where I'd gone wrong. My eyes felt heavy after doing the witchcraft, but I didn't care. Even with the lights off, I couldn't sleep. I wanted to stay awake in case something happened with Meredith.

I hugged my knees into my chest as I thought back on the past twenty-four hours. This day had sucked. Right up there with the day that I woke up in this same room seven weeks ago.

The newly replaced door opened, letting in just enough light to blind me, before it closed again. I couldn't see him, but I could smell Dastien's scent as he soundlessly made his way to my side.

He crouched in front of me, grabbing my ankle and rubbing his thumb up and down it. "Where's Max?"

"Their parents called for an update. He was upset, so he went for a walk."

He'd been really nice about everything, saying I hadn't made it any worse, but I wasn't so sure that was true. I couldn't get the image of Meredith convulsing on the roof out of my head.

"How about I take you back to your room?"

That sounded like a terrible idea. Being alone in my room when Meredith's side was empty? "No. I want to stay here. Just in case she wakes up or something."

"*Cherie.* She's not going to wake up tonight."

A tear rolled down my cheek. Would she ever wake up again?

My heart was breaking, making it hard to breathe. "I need to go back to my cousin's first thing in the morning."

"No."

"It's all we've got now. I tried…I really tried. Maybe I didn't believe in the spell enough to make it work. Maybe I wasn't strong enough." It didn't matter. I'd failed and that was all that I could think about. God. If I couldn't fix this with spells and potions, then I had to try bargaining.

"*Non. Cherie. Non. S'il vous plaît.*" His hand tightened around my ankle. "This morning I…you can't. I don't trust them. You can't go back there."

I wiped my eyes. "What else am I supposed to do? Let Meredith die?"

Dastien stood and picked me up from the chair. I was about to protest, but he sat back down with me in his lap. I curled up against him as I watched Meredith. "What did she do to deserve this?"

"All I know is that she was off campus at a field party with some of the coven a few years ago. Apparently Luciana found out about it and broke up the party."

"So other people were cursed?"

"No. Only Meredith."

Why Meredith and no one else? "What did she do?" A part of me thought it'd be easier to swallow this if I knew why it was happening. The other part of me knew that nothing would make me understand.

"Nothing to deserve this." He set me on my feet as he stood. "Come on. Let's get you to bed. You'll feel better in the morning."

"I'm scared that if I leave, she'll be gone when I wake up."

"If she gets any worse, Dr. Gonzales will come get us. Okay?"

He had a point. "Okay." I leaned down to Meredith. In the dark, her skin was so ghostly it nearly glowed. "I'm so sorry. I'll fix this. I swear. Just hang in." She was like ice. I pulled up the extra blanket that was folded at the foot of her bed, and tucked it under her chin.

"Come on, *cherie*. Let's go." His hands squeezed my shoulders as he steered me toward the door. I let him lead me out of the room.

The farther down the hallway we got, the heavier my feet were. My limbs felt like lead. "I'm exhausted," I said as I leaned into his side.

"It's been a long day."

"It feels like a million years since I woke up." It was nuts how quickly things could go wrong. My luck had always been a little on the shitty side, but this was pushing ridiculous. If it was anyone but Meredith… I wanted to stomp my foot and curse the fates.

We stepped into the still night air. The thought of going back to my room without Meredith sharing the next room hit hard.

Dastien guided me away from the dorms. "This way."

The only thing in this direction was forest and the private cabins. I'd never been to Dastien's, but we obviously weren't headed back to the dorms. The events of the day overshadowed any excitement that I normally would've felt at finally seeing his place.

The cabin was set deep in the trees. As I took in the surrounding woods, I realized that it wasn't too far from Mr. Dawson's, a little ways behind and to the right. The trees provided privacy that some of the other cabins didn't have.

The design was identical to the other ones. One-story with a porch on the front. It was all natural wood and stone colors, making it blend in with the surroundings. Dastien opened the door and waved me inside.

I was shocked that it wasn't the clichéd bachelor pad, except for a flat screen and game controllers on the coffee table. His place was spotless. If I had a pair of white gloves on, I was sure I could touch any surface in the cabin and not pick up any dirt.

The space was basically one big room. Along the back wall was a kitchen with a breakfast nook identical to Mr. Dawson's. A dark wood coffee table and a leather couch created a nice little living room nook around the TV. Along the right wall was Dastien's bed, covered in a black comforter. It was nice. Cozy. Maybe that was because it smelled like Dastien in here, like home.

"Nice place."

"Thanks."

Above the headboard were three bookshelves, which seemed a little dangerous to me, but with the limited space, I got why he'd put them there. I toed off my shoes and climbed on his bed to get a closer look. He had a lot of science fiction, but also a bunch of fantasy. Some of the same ones that I'd read. He also had a ton of non-fiction, which I usually stayed away from. Lots of psychology ones. Some texts on healing with herbs. A whole series on wildlife and survival.

I turned at the smell of beef browning. "You cook?"

He looked at me over his shoulder. "It's good to know how to make your own food when you're a werewolf. I don't know if you've noticed, but we eat a lot."

I rolled my eyes. "Yeah. I just started to notice that." I sat down on his bed and looked around. My knee bounced and I couldn't stop fidgeting with the hem of my T-shirt as I worried about Meredith. That situation was a total mess, and I had no idea where to go from there. I felt like a total failure. Helpless. Hopeless.

I pushed those thoughts away before I started crying. Wallowing in my own self-pity wouldn't help Meredith. This wasn't about me. It was about her.

I lay down on his bed, my knee still tapping out a rhythm. Being in Dastien's cabin was slightly terrifying. I wasn't scared of him, but of expectations. He was older. More experienced.

Christ. My parents would flip out if they knew I was here.

"You okay?" Dastien said from the kitchen.

I propped myself up on my elbows. "Sure." My squeaky voice was probably giving as much away as my bond was.

His brow lifted.

"I'm fine."

He didn't say anything as he considered me. We both knew I was lying.

"Sorry." I walked over to him. "Can I help?"

"Sure."

"What are you making?"

"Spaghetti. It's fast. I'd say you should go straight to sleep, but you haven't eaten in a while and you used some energy doing the spell." He pointed to a bottom cabinet. "Pot is down there."

I grabbed the pot, filled it with water, and set it on the stove to boil. That done, I hopped up on the counter to watch as he stirred a jar of sauce into the meat. It wasn't a fancy meal, but he was right—I hadn't eaten in a while.

We went through the motions of cooking, eating and cleaning up in comfortable silence. Maybe he was right and I'd wake up in the morning and have some brilliant plan.

"Go on. Get ready for bed." He handed me a T-shirt and a pair of his gym shorts.

I stepped into his bathroom and washed my face. I used my finger to brush my teeth with a little bit of his toothpaste. His clothes were ridiculous on me. The shorts hung past my knees. I tugged on the drawstring and rolled them a few times. His T-shirt was more like a dress. I laughed at myself in the mirror. But then I couldn't resist smelling the shirt. I was so keeping it.

When I came out, Dastien grinned. I shrugged. "Just because we're mates doesn't mean we're the same size."

"Thank God for that. I like that you're a little person."

I punched his arm. "I'm not a little person. I passed that status by three whole inches."

"You're my little person."

Okay. I'd give him that.

"Get in the bed. I'll take the couch." He disappeared into the bathroom. I nearly protested, but the nerves came back. He was right. Unless he was going furry, separate sleeping spaces would be good. For now.

I climbed into his bed, but it was weird being there. The scent of him filled my senses. I relaxed, and the imaginary door that kept me from getting visions disappeared. I saw night after night of him sleeping. Sometimes peacefully. Sometimes not. One time he cried.

What had made him so sad?

I was staring at the ceiling, trying to make myself fall asleep but failing, when he finally came out of the bathroom. He flicked off the light. "Goodnight, *cherie*."

"Goodnight."

I lay there for a while. Thinking about nothing and everything. I huffed. This was so pointless. There was no way I was going to sleep, and I couldn't lay here staring at the ceiling. I kicked at the sheets as I turned one way and then another, trying to find a comfortable spot. It wasn't the bed's fault. It was mine.

Resorting to counting my breaths was the only thing I could do. I finally sank into sleep, and a dream grabbed hold of me. I watched as Meredith convulsed on the roof. Only this time, after Dr. Gonzales injected her, she turned to me and said, "This is your fault."

I woke up gasping for breath in between sobs.

The mattress dipped, and Dastien pulled me toward him until we were spooning. I stiffened for a second, but the memory of the dream overwhelmed me again and I pulled him in closer to me.

He held me until I stopped crying, running his hand down my hair and brushing kisses on my head. "You're going to get through this," he whispered to me.

But I didn't want to get through it. I wanted Meredith to get through it. And for her and Donovan to have a happy life together.

I was going back to *La Alquelarre* in the morning.

"Would you rather I shift?" Dastien said.

"No." I didn't want him furry tonight. I liked being held by him. I needed that.

"Okay. Then, sleep." Dastien's command was backed with power, and I faded into a deep, dreamless sleep before I could fight it.

Chapter Thirteen

Sunlight was streaming through the curtains when I woke up. Dastien's arms were tight around me. His hot breath fanned the back of my neck. I wondered how late it was.

I searched the room for a clock, but I couldn't see one from where I was. Why didn't he have an alarm clock?

"It's still early," Dastien said from behind me.

I froze for a second. "Did I wake you?"

"In a way. I felt your bond go crazy with worry."

"Do you always feel when I wake up?"

He pressed a kiss to the back of my neck. "You didn't know you were my alarm clock?"

I grinned. "What did you do before me?"

"I set the alarm on my phone. But now, when I'm not in your bed as a wolf, I don't need one. I know when you wake up, and I get ready so I can meet you for breakfast."

I thought about it for a second. "I can't tell if that's uber creepy or kind of sweet…I'm leaning toward creepy."

"That's the second time in twenty-four hours that you've called me creepy. What's so wrong with wanting to have breakfast with you?" He squeezed me tighter.

"What time is it?"

He rolled over and grabbed his cell. "Nine."

"Any word about Meredith?"

"No."

I had to stay calm. No news was good news. "I'm going to throw on my clothes from yesterday and then I'm going to see her."

"Hey," Dastien said, holding onto my hand before I could fully roll out of bed.

"What?"

"I really liked having you here."

On any other day, when I wasn't about to go beg for my friend's life, I would've wanted to linger in bed and enjoy being there. But I couldn't afford the time. "I liked being here."

I headed to the bathroom and splashed water on my face. I looked like hell and could really use a shower, but there wasn't time. This would have to do. I pulled on my jeans and T-shirt and knotted my hair in a messy top-bun.

When I stepped out, Dastien was dressed. Old faded jeans and a nondescript gray T-shirt. A pair of cheap foam flip-flops. Fighting clothes. All stuff that could be easily discarded.

I wondered what he was planning on doing today.
"I'll go with you. The rest of Meredith's family should be here."

God. It probably was a crappy idea to go see her if they were there.

"They don't blame you. They can't. You didn't do this to her, and accepting responsibility for something that happened years ago, before you even knew Meredith, is silly." He paused to let that sink in, and it did. I don't know why I felt like it was my fault, but it really, truly felt like it was. "If you want to see her, then let's go."

I nodded. He held my hand as we walked back across campus. This was one of those times when I appreciated that we could not talk and be fine. His support meant a lot.

The infirmary was quiet when we got there. Outside Meredith's door, Shannon stood talking softly to three tall blonde guys—Meredith's other brothers. I weaved my way through the crowd with Dastien a step behind me.

When Shannon spotted us, her face reddened. "What're you doing here?"

"I want to see her."

"You shouldn't be here. This is your fault."

Dastien's anger hit me through our bond. "It's not her fault."

"Yes, it is. It's both your faults."

"How do you figure that?" I said. Sure, I messed up last night, but the rest of it... Dastien was right. I couldn't accept responsibility for something I didn't do.

"If you hadn't bit her, none of this would've happened."

"How can you—" Dastien said, but Shannon cut him off.

"No. You don't get it. You weren't there at the party. I was. Luciana had been getting visions for years—*years*—about losing a key coven member to the wolves, but she didn't know who it'd be. So when she got to the party and saw Daniel making out with Meredith, she flipped. But it wasn't Daniel who was going to get bit. It was *you*."

Shit. Oh, holy shit. "But I didn't know—"

"You will stop right there," Dastien said. "If that's what happened, then clearly Luciana saw things and she acted irrationally. There's nothing in this world that could've stopped me from biting my own mate. We all know that fighting destiny—fighting fate—never turns out well. The only one to blame is Luciana. She's the one who did this."

He stepped toward Shannon. "You've lashed out at my mate for the last time. Blaming her for stealing me, her own mate. For hurting Meredith. For any little thing you don't like. I won't have it anymore."

"She wasted time! She could've spent time trying to free Meredith's wolf, but she didn't. She could've agreed to stay with the coven, but she didn't. That's twice she could've saved Meredith and she didn't do it. Twice!"

The hallway was beyond quiet, everyone else would've had to leave the building to not hear this fight.

I wanted to crawl in a hole, but I couldn't. "She's right."

Dastien spun to face me. "No. She's not."

"No. I could do something, and I haven't." I let out a breath. "I'm so sorry," I said to her brothers. The door to Meredith's room opened and her parents and Max stepped out.

"This isn't your doing," her father said.

"No. But I can put it right. I can get Luciana to let go of her curse, and that will let Meredith's wolf free." Dastien's fear and rage took my breath away. He'd never let me, but I had to. "I'll go back and talk to the coven. Make a trade, myself for Meredith, and she'll fix it. I—"

"*Non.*"

"*Oui,*" I said in my best French accent.

"*Non, cherie! Non.*" He started rattling off in French. Meredith's family and Shannon started arguing, too. I closed my eyes as I tried to figure out what I was doing. For the first time in twenty-four hours, the weight lifted. This was the right thing. I needed to go back to *La Aquelarre.*

154

But this time, I wanted back-up.

"Aaaand," I said talking over everyone, "I'd like you to come with me, Dastien."

His eyes turned from amber to golden. "That's a terrible idea. You think things can't get worse but they will if we show up on the coven's land together."

Manipulating him was wrong, but my options were limited. "Then I'll go alone."

"The hell you will." His voice was nearly full-growl as he shook my shoulders.

"Just hear me out."

"You have about thirty seconds before I lock you in the feral cages."

What? The guy had lost his mind if he was threatening me with the cages. They were below the gym, and made of concrete and steel. It was a place where they put wolves when they were out of control.

But he was seriously threatening to lock me up? "I don't think I can live with myself if I don't go and try to work something out, but I'm in a little over my head." I took a calming breath, and hoped Dastien would listen to reason. "You're right. I shouldn't trust Luciana. She's not a good person, but maybe we can reach a compromise. I'd be happy to go there a couple of days a week to learn their ways or whatever, if they agree to undo the curse on Meredith. It'd be good stuff to learn anyway. And maybe I can find someone to take over the coven in my place. Help me make a fair bargain with her."

"It's dangerous. Luciana's already proven she's willing to curse you, too," Dastien said.

Meredith's mother gasped. Her curls bounced as she turned to me. "If they did it once, they could do it again."

"They only cursed me to make me go back." I sighed.

"I get everyone's concern, but I can do this. I did my best using what I know about witchcraft and I failed. This is the only other option. Meredith's dying."

My voice cracked and I paused. They had to agree with me. Losing my cool wasn't going to help me argue my point. "They're not going to hurt me when I'm what they want in the end. If I bring anyone, Luciana might try something, but she can't do much to Dastien. He's too powerful and too high up in the pack. And he's my mate. They know they can't touch Dastien if they have any chance of keeping me around." I gripped his hand. "If I can get them to agree to one or two days a week on coven land, then that's a small price to pay for Meredith's life."

Meredith's shortest brother cleared his throat. He didn't look much older than us. "I think she's got a point. They're not going to hurt her. And if she's willing to take the risk to save our sister, we shouldn't turn her down." He met my gaze. "We all want Meredith alive and healthy."

I nodded. "I'm willing to give it a try, but I need Dastien."

When I looked at him, Dastien closed his eyes and when they opened again, they were still glowing gold. "Okay. We can go, but at the first sign of trouble, we're getting the hell out of there. And I get to say what you agree to. If I don't like it, we leave."

I usually wouldn't let him be the boss, but I was too afraid of agreeing to something I shouldn't. I was desperate, and they'd know that. It was really easy to take advantage of the hopeless. "Deal."

He rested his forehead against mine. "For the record, I think this is a bad idea. Luciana could've done the right thing and fixed this yesterday morning, but she didn't."

"I know. Believe me, I'm aware. I'm not letting my

guard down." I leaned away from him.

"Let's go, before I change my mind," Dastien said.

Max stepped toward me. "Thank you."

"No more thank yous from you. Let's see if I can actually do this first."

"No, he's right," Shannon said. "Thank you for finally doing the right thing."

That was a backhanded comment if I ever heard one, but now that I knew both reasons why Shannon hated me, she'd be easier to handle. Dastien had crushed a lot of girl's hearts when he bit me, but we were mates. It was fate. Now she wanted to hold me responsible for Meredith's curse, too?

It was easier to hate me instead of dealing with what was going on, but that wasn't exactly fair. I didn't curse Meredith—Luciana did. Once Meredith was better, maybe she'd know how to smooth things over between me and Shannon, but not right now.

I gave her a small nod, and then started back the way we came.

"Should we call someone? Tell them that we're coming?" I asked Dastien.

He shook his head. "Usually, I'd arrange a neutral ground to meet them on, but that would give them a chance to prepare. So, we're just going to show up."

"And hope for the best."

He smiled but his dimples didn't show. "*Oui.* And hope for the best."

***

The second time passing through the gate was easier. I was prepared for that slimy feeling as Dastien drove his car over the cattle guard.

"Did you feel it?" I asked.

Dastien glanced at me briefly before turning back to the road. "Not like you did, but I could feel your disgust."

Right. "I'm not sure which house is Luciana's. Just park wherever."

He found an empty spot between a beat-up looking truck and a Prius. I stepped out of the car, not sure what my plan was. Hell, who was I kidding? There was no real plan.

Three people came out of a house down the road. Two guys and one girl. One of the guys was Daniel.

I blocked the sun with my hand as they walked toward us. I wasn't sure if I should walk up to him or what, but he took the choice away from me.

He said something so softly to the others that I couldn't hear, and then started toward me. The other two headed for the house across the road.

Here we go.

Daniel wore a pair of khaki shorts and a blue T-shirt with something printed on it. A band name? Not my kind of music, so I wasn't sure. His hair was wet, like he'd just showered, and smelled of tea tree oil shampoo.

"Hi, Daniel," I said when he got close.

"Teresa."

I ground my teeth at the use of my name.

"What are you doing back here?" His eyebrows were drawn down. He wasn't scowling, per se, but he didn't look sure about me either. Daniel glanced over my shoulder at Dastien for a second before meeting my gaze again.

"I wanted to talk to Luciana about Meredith. I was hoping to come to an arrangement."

"And you brought *him* with you?"

I didn't like how he said that. Dastien stood a few feet behind me and a little to the left. His arms were loose at his sides, knees slightly bent. It was a protective posture. He was watching Daniel's movements, ready to pounce if he needed to, and he was far enough to the side not to have to bump into me to do it.

"Yes," I said. "We're a package deal these days."

Daniel crossed his arms. He was scowling now. "You weren't supposed to be."

Dastien growled and I shot him a look. "Cool it."

He huffed, cutting off the growl, but his eyes stayed glowing gold and I had a feeling he wouldn't be covering them with sunglasses.

This wasn't going well and we'd only been here a couple minutes.

Daniel glanced at me. "You know, I always felt bad about what happened to Meredith. She didn't deserve that. My mom threw the potion and said the incantation so fast I didn't even know what she'd done. One second we were making out, the next Meredith was on the ground screaming like someone had died. I'll never forget that sound. It was horrible." He shuddered. "I hear your visions are much stronger than what my mom sees, but you get past and present stuff, while she gets impressions of the future. Only it's never specific enough to do any real good. Basically all she got was that someone in the coven was going to be getting hot and heavy with a wolf, and would get turned. That's why she freaked."

Which had been me. Not Daniel.

Still, why keep Meredith under the curse? Why continue to punish her for something she didn't do? "But Meredith didn't bite you, so why didn't she reverse it?"

"Because she's gone anti-wolf. She's always been anti-anything we're not, but since she had that vision, she's been a little out of control. Even more so since you were bitten. It's kind of an obsession. So why would she reverse it?"

A door slammed up the road, and a woman screamed. "Stay away from my son!"

Luciana came running from a house down the road. She waved her hands, saying something that I couldn't hear, but apparently Daniel knew what she was doing.

"No. Mom!" He stepped in front of me. He stumbled back a few steps, as if something punched him. "Stay behind me. Both of you."

"I don't need your protection." Dastien bit the words out. "But your mother might if she tries that again."

My skin itched to go wolf. This was so beyond dangerous it wasn't even funny. It'd be a miracle if we got out of here without starting a war.

"I came to bargain," I said.

She slowed her run to a fast walk. "Seeing things my way?"

I shook my head. "No, but I want to save a good friend. An innocent girl."

Luciana scoffed. "She's not innocent. None of the wolves are."

Dastien started to growl and I elbowed him. I instantly regretted it. It was like hitting granite. I rubbed my elbow, trying to gain the feeling back.

"If you release Meredith from whatever was done to her, I'll come here one day a week to study."

Luciana shook her head. "No. You stay here. For good. I suppress your wolf, and I'll put Meredith's back to sleep so she can live."

I tried to maintain my cool, but I could feel Dastien's bubbling anger bleeding through our bond. "That's not a compromise."

"Did I say I wanted to compromise?"

I had to calm down. I took a moment to look around the compound. A few people gathered on the street to watch us talk. More people were staring through windows.

I raised my voice as I spoke, hoping that if Luciana wasn't going to listen to what I was saying, maybe someone else here would. "You can't expect to lead if you're not willing to compromise."

"I don't negotiate with monsters."

Rage rippled along my skin. "You're killing an innocent girl and you dare call me—us—monsters." Three calming breaths were all I allowed myself. "Meredith Molloney is the true mate of Donovan Murrey. One of the Seven. Killing her will win you no friends. Are you and your people prepared to make enemies of all the wolves? Not just this pack, but every pack? You wanted me here, so here I am. I'm offering one day a week in exchange for you to release Meredith from the curse."

"No."

Murmers went around the group. Some of the coven members looked wary.

Daniel put his hand on his mother's shoulder. "We should accept her offer. Having Donovan as an enemy is not an option."

"No," Luciana said. "She needs to let go of her wolf and take her place in the coven."

"I can't do that." Taking my wolf away was not an option, and Luciana was crazy for thinking it was. "It'd be like cutting off one of my legs just for the hell of it. I'm not doing it. I'm a wolf and a witch—equal halves of both. You don't have the right or the power to separate me from my wolf."

"If you were so powerful, you'd be able to break the cage Meredith's wolf is in," Luciana said. "But you can't even see it to break it. You can't even find it. That's not power."

Break the cage? *See* it?

Break the cage. I could find it?

That was it. Holy shit. Luciana gave me what I needed.

I was a combination of wolf and witch. I combined alpha powers with witchcraft. I hadn't learned much about either, but I knew that my alpha powers gave me control. And control was what I needed to guide my witchcraft.

Donovan hadn't been talking about merging types of witchcraft. He'd been talking about me specifically mixing my witchcraft with my alpha energy. Just like I'd done to contact him.

Oh my God.

Shannon and Chris had been right all along. I could break the curse. I'd just been thinking about it the wrong way. I'd been looking at it from either an alpha way—by getting an alpha strong enough to calm her wolf—or a witchcraft way—by using spells and potions to get her wolf to settle down.

In the middle of this fight with Luciana, I was instantly calm.

A smile spread across my face. Meredith's wolf was locked up. Chained inside her. All I had to do was find the cage with my witchcraft, and help her break it and call her wolf forward by using alpha powers. And if I didn't have enough alpha energy, I could pull it from the pack.

It all made sense now. I just hadn't seen it before.

I'd been running from the wolf stuff since I became a

wolf and it was high time I embraced it along with my *bruja* side.

Luciana was still rambling on, but nothing she said mattered anymore. I wasn't listening.

"Goodbye, Luciana." She stopped talking to stare at me. "Turns out, I don't need your help. And you've just made an enemy for life." I turned my back, trusting Daniel and Dastien to keep watch. "Let's go."

I grabbed the keys from Dastien and hopped in the car. I floored it through the gate. The burn on the way out barely registered.

"You've got a plan."

I nodded. "Yes. Call the school. I need every wolf in the area in the courtyard by the time we get there. Everyone you can find. All the Cazadores. Everyone."

"On it." He pulled his cell phone from his pocket, and started making calls.

This could work. Holy shit. This could be it.

Chapter Fourteen

Dastien's phone worked overtime for nearly the whole car ride. We knew our time was limited. He checked in with Dr. Gonzales and she said Meredith was still alive, but had only an hour or two left.

I sped down the road, not caring about getting a ticket. There was no slowing down.

When Dastien was done with his calls, we were minutes away from campus.

"What's the plan?"

I tapped my fingers along the steering wheel. "I'm going to need your help. I don't really know what I'm doing, but I have a theory."

He turned to face me. "Tell me."

I glanced at him for a second before turning back to the road. "You can make me change if you wanted to."

"Yes. I could."

"You could make just about anyone, right?"

"Yes."

"Even if they didn't want to."

"*Oui*. Of course. Yes." He paused. "I think I know

where you're going with this, but I already tried that with Meredith... Actually, I tried to calm her wolf. Waking it up would only hurt her worse."

"See, that's what I thought too. But Luciana talked about the curse like she trapped Meredith's wolf in a cage, and all I had to do was release her. I think if I connect with Meredith again so that I can 'see' Meredith's wolf, and then I use witchcraft and break the cage while I use alpha power to force the change, then the cage will crumble. The curse will break." I was on to something. If Dastien agreed, this could really be it. "You weren't enough on your own to affect her change, but if we got enough of us together, I think we could make it work."

"I don't know. It makes sense in theory, but do you think you can connect with her enough to see that?"

I hoped so. "I saw all kinds of stuff when I was with her. Memories after she first changed. With her brothers. Hanging out with her mom. I think I can get to her, and once I do, it'll be about timing. It'll take some doing, but I think we can." I paused.

"This could work. It's just... Shit," he said as his phone rang. He switched to French, talking for a few minutes before hanging up.

I pulled into the big black gates at St. Ailbe's. The lot was completely full. Cars were blocking others in and there was no hope of finding a place to park. I didn't look for one. Instead, I drove up the path that led to school.

There were people milling around. As soon as they saw me, they stopped and stared.

Jeeze. Enough with the staring already.

Dastien nodded at them when we got out and they headed off without a word.

"Everyone's in the courtyard. Go get Meredith and

bring her."

Dastien took off sprinting, and I ran the other direction. When I got to the end of the path, the trees cleared and I stopped.

Where had Dastien found all these people? There had to be six or seven hundred. Our school had barely three hundred. I swallowed. It seemed a little odd that the newbie wolf was going to use all of them, but I could do this. At least I thought I could.

My gaze darted from face to face as I started toward the crowd.

One by one, people started muttering and pointing my way. I was sure that with the way the St. Ailbe's rumor mill worked, everyone here knew who I was. I wasn't sure if that made me uncomfortable or more confident. Probably the former.

They made way for me as I stepped into the middle of the clearing.

I spotted a familiar head of wavy blond hair and met Chris' gaze. Shannon was next to him with all four of Meredith's brothers. They nodded at me, and I tried to look confident—chin up, back straight—but I wasn't sure if I pulled it off at all.

Adrian was standing beside Meredith's brothers. He stuck his thumb up in the air with a grin.

Good God. How was he smiling when Meredith was barely alive?

If I couldn't pull this one off...

Rosa's words came back to me, and I pushed my fears aside. Confidence. And light. Put my faith, my will, my heart into the work. I had love for Meredith. I'd connect with her, and free the wolf from her cage.

Butterflies took flight in my stomach as I waited. I tried

not to worry about everyone watching me. I was used to being watched. I could do this.

Dastien stepped into the circle everyone had formed around me with Meredith in his arms. She moaned.

No. This wasn't good. "Is she awake?"

He placed her down gently. "Yes. She's burning the drugs off faster than we can give them to her. At least we won't have to fight the drugs and the curse to get her awake."

Dr. Gonzales was right behind him. "When you're ready, I'll give her a shot to wake her up a little more. I don't want her to get sick or convulse, but I think we'll want her a bit more alert."

I wanted to say no freaking way was she giving her anything to wake her up, but that was my fear talking. I couldn't bring fear into this. I needed to be firm. My visions would guide me to her, and my alpha powers would help her escape. "Okay."

Her parents stepped into the circle. Her mother squeezed me tight. "Thank you."

God. I wished everyone would stop thanking me. I hadn't done anything yet.

The pressure made my chest tight.

Dastien moved to my side. "Thank you so much for coming. My mate and I think that together as a pack, we can break through what's been holding Meredith's wolf at bay." His voice was clear and confident. "It might leave everyone here drained, but as you can see, it's a worthy cause."

He squeezed my hand. "Do you want to say anything?"

I shook my head. Was he nuts? No, I didn't want to say anything.

Wait. Yes, I did. "Meredith has been a good friend to

me, no questions asked. I'm going to try and repay the favor, and I need everyone's help. I know I drained a lot of you yesterday, and I really appreciate you being up to trying it again. I'm doing something different this time, though. I'm hoping it's enough to break the curse." I looked at Dr. Gonzales.

She knelt by Meredith's side, and waited for my signal.

Dastien pressed a kiss to my forehead.

My heart was racing as I sat by Meredith.

I took a breath, and grasped Meredith's hand in my own. Her fingers felt like a bunch of brittle sticks. I swallowed and looked at Dr. Gonzales. She plunged the needle into Meredith's other arm.

Meredith's eyelids fluttered for a few seconds before opening.

"You ready?" Dastien asked.

"Yeah." I hoped so. I let down every barrier I had. "Meredith."

She moaned.

"Show me your wolf."

I was in the field of bluebonnets again. The sun was brighter. It was earlier in the day. She was with her brother in human form. Meredith looked younger without her dyed hair, but she was definitely a teenager. She was wearing a flower printed dress—which was so nothing Meredith would ever wear.

"You're going to be fine. I'm going to shift, and you just follow my lead, okay?"

"No, Max! Don't—"

Max laughed, and quicker than I could blink, he was on four legs with his clothes piled at his feet. He butted his head against her legs.

"Cut it out."

When she went to push him away, he nipped her hand. "Ouch. You son of a bitch! That hurt!" And then fur rippled along her arms. Her change was slower than his. It took maybe five seconds instead of milliseconds.

"Meredith! Show me where she is!"

I knew my wolf hid in the center of myself. The first week I'd turned, Dastien taught me how to picture her and become more at one with that side of myself. He said most Weres inherently knew how to do that, but the whole having a wolf sharing your space was a bit of a game changer for me.

I expected the bright light to blind me like last time. To see the image flare bright and then dim again, but it didn't. Instead, the wolf in my vision turned to me, and plopped down on her bottom. She howled. It was so loud, I had to cover my ears.

And then I was plunged into darkness. The field, flowers, and daylight were gone. I held out my hand in front of my face and couldn't see it.

A wolf whined, and I stepped toward it, waving my arms around trying to feel for it.

I hit a soft mass, and fell over her. "Sorry," I said as the wolf whined.

Hope blossomed. I couldn't believe I'd actually found her wolf. This might totally work.

I still couldn't see, but I felt around her. She was covered in chains. I pulled at them, but there was no way I could break them. They didn't even budge.

Okay. So this was it. I'd found her. Now I had to send my strength to Meredith's wolf so she could grow stronger and break out of the cage.

That would take alpha powers.

I reached for my bond to Dastien and mentally tugged

at it. Strength and power flowed into me. His focus and determination became my own.

And then it hit me so hard that I felt like I was drowning. So much power.

Before, when I'd been in Meredith's room talking to Donovan, I hadn't known what I was doing. I hadn't been aware of the power rolling through me, but now I was. I could feel each wolf. The essence of everyone present.

"You're going to be fine, Meredith. Take what's offered." I closed my eyes, and pictured the energy flowing directly into her wolf. I harnessed the will to change. "Shift, Meredith." I said, using all the power that I could. "Shift now." I pulled on the chains around her wolf with the strength of the pack.

Her hand jerked.

I opened my eyes and found myself in the real world. She hadn't shifted. I had to go back in. I gripped her hand in mine, holding tight, and I closed my eyes again.

I was back in the darkness and felt the chains under my hands.

Grabbing all the power I could, I pulled on them.

"Chains, break!" I put some of my witchy powers into the words, forcing my will into them. It didn't matter what I said, only the intention. I pictured them breaking and yanked again, and they creaked against each other.

"Now. Meredith. Change now. Do it. Now!"

The power was building. Burning through me like a fire in the depths of my soul. I pushed it toward her.

I pulled on the chains. "Break. Now. Break." They creaked again. "Change now! Do it now! Shift!"

I alternated pushing alpha energy at Meredith and using witchcraft to weaken the chains.

Howls echoed along the pack bonds. The wolves were

all shifting, but Meredith wasn't.

I put my will and faith behind my words. "Break!" I tugged on the chains, and felt a link break. They were loosening.

I grabbed more power from the pack. "Shift!" I was screaming now.

Another link cracked, and the chains gave even more.

"Shift now!" I yelled, pushing more alpha power.

I heard Dastien's howl through the bond. I wasn't sure how I could distinguish his from the others, but I knew it was him. He'd shifted along with the others, which meant I was reaching the end of the line of power.

More wolves howled.

"Break! Chains break!" I pulled on the chains and they broke. I lost my balance and fell, sprawling on my back.

White light blinded me.

I opened my eyes, back in the real world.

The white wolf from my vision sat in front of me. Meredith. She looked up to the sky and howled.

Oh my God. I'd done it. Meredith was a wolf, and she was okay. She was really okay.

Hot tears rolled down my cheeks as I laughed. "God. Took you forever, chica."

Wolf-Meredith whimpered.

Thank God. She was okay.

The fear for her melted away. I had a second to enjoy it before pain rolled through my limbs and another fear replaced it.

I wasn't okay.

I screamed, trying to hold my shape, but I couldn't.

Fur rippled along my skin as my own wolf started to take over. My knees popped.

Oh God. No. Not yet. I wasn't ready.

I squeezed my eyes shut as another ripple of pain moved through my muscles as they reformed.

Dastien's wolf nose touched the back of my neck, urging me to keep going.

"No. I can't." My voice was gravelly. I fought against my wolf. Terror clawed along my spine. I wasn't ready for this. I had two more days before I had to do this.

I felt a strong alpha energy closing in fast. The rest of the wolves must've felt it, too because they started howling.

It was too much. Too loud. I couldn't fight it all.

"Move out of the way," Donovan said.

Oh God. He was the Alpha I was feeling. He'd force my change. I couldn't let him, but I was shaking from pain and the need to go furry.

"Shift!" The command hit me with a force so strong, it took my breath away.

The wolves howled as one.

I groaned, but there was no stopping it. My strength was waning. "No. Please." My muscles fought against me, but I was holding off the change. I screamed, stuck between forms.

"You're a damned stubborn one." Donovan stood above me. His blue eyes bright. "You saved my mate, and I'll not have you hurting like this. You listen to my command and you follow it. Do you understand?"

"No. I can't," my voice was low and scratchy.

"You will." He put his hand on my forehead. "Shift now, Teresa Elizabeth McCaide."

So much power. So much force. I couldn't fight it anymore.

It was as if a dam inside me broke. My form was fluid. One second I was in pain, on the ground, struggling to maintain my sanity as my clothes were shredding. The next

I was on my side and everything was calm. For the first time since I woke up at St. Ailbe's, I felt completely at peace.

My vision changed. It wasn't in black and white, but it was muted. And my sense of smell. If I'd thought I could smell everything before, I could smell more now. Every little thing. The grass. The dirt. The bugs crawling between the two. I jumped up to my feet. All four of them. Weird. I stumbled for a second. And then turned to find Meredith.

She was a beautiful white wolf. She sat with Donovan's arms around her. "Why didn't you tell me that this was the reason you refused me? We could've fixed this together. It didn't have to be a no," Donovan said to her. "God. I don't think I've ever been so terrified. Never scare me like that again. Never. You got me?"

Meredith whimpered, and I laughed. It came out like a chuffing sound.

I looked around the circle. The wolves were there. Watching. I howled, and they answered in unison.

The pack bond wove through each of them. Some weaker than others. Some burning bright.

Dastien howled twice, and the wolves scattered into the woods. Then he rubbed his side against mine and took off running.

Where the hell was he going?

I took off. Chasing him. I stumbled and tripped a bit before figuring out where my new shape was in space. My claws dug into the dirt as I moved.

I got caught up in the new sensations of the world around me. It took me a bit to realize I'd totally lost Dastien.

What the hell? Where did he go?

I sat down and whined. This was bullshit.

He crashed through the bushes at me, and I rolled. He motioned toward the ground with his nose, then took off.

Oh. I was supposed to smell. Right.

In my new form, my sense of smell was almost as good as my sight. I could tell how long it'd been since an animal had passed by, but since it was all new, I wasn't sure what each scent was.

As we ran and played, I got a sense of freedom. Occasionally I'd catch a whiff of something yum, but when I'd see it was a bunny or a bird, I'd leave it alone.

I had a feeling if Dastien was alone, he would've made it his prey, but I wasn't there yet. I wasn't sure I'd ever be there.

But Meredith was fine. I was fine.

Hell, I was more than fine. I was a fucking wolf.

After a little while, my stomach growled. Dastien gave his wolf-y laugh, and led me to a bush. A small black plastic bin was hidden under some leaves. He left me there.

So I was supposed to change. How the hell did that happen? I went behind another bush and squeezed my eyes shut, hoping that I would magically turn back to human.

Nope, still furry.

Oh shit. I was stuck. I was going to be a wolf forever.

Damn it. This was so not cool.

Chapter Fifteen

Dastien's laughter echoed through the woods. He was hiccupping he was laughing so hard.

Dude better watch himself. I had some nasty teeth in this form.

His laughter died. I heard the sound of the plastic bin opening and something being unzipped. "You're not stuck," he said. "Just picture yourself in human form, and you'll change."

Oh crap. Could he hear what I was thinking now?

"Yeah."

Not cool.

"Come on. It's kind of cool."

Stalker. Creepo.

"I'm not a creepo. I'm your mate. It's like the visions though. You can block it whenever you want. You're just shouting your thoughts really loudly right now."

He squatted beside me, now wearing a pair of gray sweatpants, and took my face in his hands. "Do it, Tess. Picture yourself on two feet and you will be." He ran his hands through the fur along my sides and I pretty much started purring. "You pulled so much power, you've got to be starving. We could've hunted and stayed to play as wolves, but you didn't want any of the rabbits."

I growled. I was really hungry, but biting into a bloody, furry bunny didn't sound the least bit appealing.

"Right. Let's not forget where the meat you eat comes from."

He had a point, but I didn't want to kill it myself. And bunnies were too cute to eat.

He patted my side. "Come on. I'll give you some space." He put a pair of sweatpants and a T-shirt on the ground beside me. "Do what I said. Don't freak out. Don't pick it apart. Do it." He walked away to give me privacy.

Fine. I was going to do it.

I closed my eyes and pictured my hands. Five fingers. My arms. My legs. My feet. And suddenly I was me again.

It went so fast, it didn't even hurt. I patted my body to make sure everything was where it was supposed to be. No more fur. No more paws. Two arms, two legs. No tail. I really was me again. "Thank God." I relaxed against the ground.

"Are you dressed?"

"No!" No, I wasn't. "No peeking!"

I pulled on the T-shirt and sweatpants. They were way too big. I was smaller than everyone at the school by at least half a foot. Even the girls. I rolled up the bottoms of the pants and tightened the drawstring.

Before I could do anything, Dastien pressed me against the tree. "I'm so proud of you."

"I didn't do it by myself."

"No. But you did it. And I'm glad you changed."

"Eh. It wasn't so bad."

His answering grin made my legs weak. His dimples

appeared, like magic, showing me how happy he was. He leaned in, brushing my lips softly with his before pulling away. "*Je t'aime, cherie,*" he said before kissing me deeply.

We slid to the ground. I couldn't take my eyes from him as I tried to catch my breath. I licked my lips and stared at him.

God. He was way too hot. His abs. His long, muscular legs. His arms. Holy shit, his arms.

I was addicted to him. Totally and completely.

It occurred to me that he took great care of me, minus the whole biting thing, but what did I do for him? He balanced me. Brought me back whenever I was losing control. He was fun. He made me laugh and relax. He didn't take anything too seriously, except for the Cazadores and the pack. And me.

Dastien sat up on his elbows. "What is it?"

I raised an eyebrow in question.

"You blocked me when you changed forms, so I can't read you. But I can still feel your emotions and you're full of doubts. What are you thinking?"

"Don't make me say it. Just let me have a little privacy." Man, he always wanted to talk about it. I could already tell he wasn't going to let this one go.

"No way. Not when you're feeling like that." He pulled me closer. "That's why I like the walls down. So you don't hide things from me."

My cheeks were on fire. "It's nothing." I hopped up, but he snatched my foot and I fell to the ground a few feet from him.

I screeched—a very uncool sound—and tried to stop myself as he dragged me back to him. It was a lost cause, and I wasn't sure I wanted to win anyhow.

When I was close, he pounced on me, pinning me to

the ground. "You sure you don't want to tell me?"

I nodded.

His eyes flashed amber and he dug his fingers into my side, tickling me. I started convulsing with laughter.

He stopped. "And now?"

"No way. I'm not—"

I was laughing again. Gasping for air. I threw my weight around, trying to get out from under him, but I was fully pinned. There would be no breaking free.

"Now?"

"No way."

He found the right spot, along my second rib. I don't know why it was so damned ticklish there, but I couldn't breathe I was laughing so hard. Tears rolled down my cheeks.

"Uncle. Uncle!" I shouted when I thought I might pee my pants if he didn't stop.

He sat back on his heels and pulled me to sit. "And?"

It took me a second to catch my breath. "I was just..." Damn it. I wiped my hands down my face, and tried to untangle my hair but it was a lost cause and I had no hair tie.

Crap. This was beyond embarrassing. "I was wondering what our relationship did for you?"

The surprised laugh that came from Dastien made me want to crawl in a deep dark hole. "You what?" He yell-laughed.

I mumbled something incoherent and he laughed harder. It echoed through the woods and he fell on his back.

Screw this. I was being serious and he was laughing at me. "You're an ass." I got up and kicked his side.

Before I could turn to walk away, he snagged my foot

again, and pulled me down on him. "You're everything to me."

I tried to sit back, but he wouldn't let me.

"Please. Just listen. Don't think too much about it or worry or pick it apart like I know you do."

"I don't do that." It was a total lie.

He brushed the hair back from my face as I stared down at him. "Yes, you do. I can feel your worry. I might not know exactly what you're thinking right now, but I can feel you go into yourself and dissect everything."

Crap. This was only going to get worse when we finished the bond in two freaking days. I blew out a breath. "So why are you with me? Why did you pick me? You're handsome and kind and thoughtful and giving and patient. And I'm just…I'm me."

He muttered something in French, but I poked him.

"That sure sounds pretty, but I don't understand a word of it."

"We'll have to get you speaking French. It's much easier to romance someone in a love language." He pinched my nose. "You think I was like this with everyone?"

"You were. When I first got here, everyone, especially the girls, thought I'd ruined their perfect Dastien."

"I'm not perfect." He sighed. "I think you've built this up in your head and you're not seeing yourself clearly. Or us clearly."

I rested my cheek on his chest. "I think it's hard because I didn't know you before. I only know you now."

"Hmm," he said. His chest rumbled under me, and I relaxed. "I've said it before, that I was restless, but I guess no one else saw that. I wasn't happy. I felt alone, and it put me on edge. Not because I was alone, I had friends, but because I had too much power. I didn't have to listen to what Michael said. I didn't have to obey anyone—except maybe Donovan and Sebastian."

He ran his hand lazily up and down my spine as he spoke. It made me want to purr with contentment. "For some, it might've been fun, but for me, that meant that I had to watch myself. I had to control my emotions. Everyone is responsible for their own actions, but as werewolves, there's a bit of comfort knowing that while you're trying to settle into your wolf, that someone is always above you and can keep you in check or help you when you feel out of control. I didn't have that safety net."

I sat up to look him in the eyes. "But that's not anything I can do for you."

"Yes, you can. You don't realize the strength within you. Now that you've shifted, you'll feel it more."

I rolled my eyes at that bit of nonsense. "I'm not stronger than you."

"I think you might be. Not everyone would handle the change so well. Not just anyone could even survive it. And no one—no one—could've done what you did today. You saved her, *cherie*."

Dastien ran his hand up and down my spine, and I wanted to lay there with him forever.

"Everything happened fast with us and it's been an exceptionally rough couple of days. We haven't spent enough time talking about what's going to happen this weekend, and that's my fault. I'd give you more time, but we need to formally finish the bonding before the Tribunal."

"I know. This thing with Meredith was scary, but it also was a distraction. Now I'm going back to being worried about what's going to happen."

"We're mates. Two halves. They can't separate us. I won't let them." He paused. "You asked me what you do for me. Well, you balance me. I never laughed this much before you came into my life. Sure, you get into crazy situations, but I like being there for you. It makes me happy and keeps things interesting. I like that I can do things for you. Sharing my life with you is like the best Christmas present ever. Don't doubt what we have."

I squeezed my eyes shut. "You wouldn't rather be with someone who was a super awesome fighter?"

"Do you want to be a super awesome fighter?"

"No." He knew I didn't. We'd been practicing, and I was getting decent, but it wasn't a passion of mine. "I don't want to get bitten by a vamp again, but I don't want to be a Cazador."

"I've done enough fighting for the both of us, and I'll continue to do it because I like it. But that doesn't mean you have to. We might be mates, but we don't have to do everything the same. That would be boring."

I snorted. "Thanks."

"*De rien.* Are you feeling better about us now?"

I took a second to listen to his calm, steady heartbeat. "I think so. Yeah."

"In two nights we're having the ceremony. It's not a wedding, but it's as good as one in the pack."

I narrowed my gaze. "Don't you think you should've asked me something first?"

His nose scrunched for a second. "I kind of skipped that part when I bit you."

I poked his stomach. "Well, I'm still a traditional, ex-human girl."

"I'm aware. When the Tribunal is done, we'll do things the way a traditional, ex-human girl would want. Even the ring part."

I was liking the sound of this. "The ring part?"

He grinned. "I have one for you."

"Can I have it now?" I held out my hand with a grin.

"I don't have it on me," he said with a laugh, and I shoved him into the ground.

Dastien shook his head.

"Fine. But you need a ring too. It's more than a piece of jewelry. It's a sign to everyone else that you're off the market."

"Don't worry. Everyone will know you're taken." He pulled me down to him.

I nipped his neck. "That wasn't what I was worried about."

He was smiling when he said, "They'll know that I'm taken too." I melted into him. His tongue brushed against my lips, and I opened. Heat swamped me. I wrapped my legs around his waist, and ran my fingers through his hair. My hips rocked, and he groaned. I couldn't stop the motion. My need for him was so strong, I couldn't breathe.

He rolled until I was on the ground. His weight was on his forearms, but every bit of his body was against mine. He reached up, palming my breast, and my own moan slipped free, causing me to break the kiss. He licked my neck before placing a soft kiss just below my ear.

"We have to stop this," he said.

"No," I said, trying to pull his face back to mine.

He sat up after a second. "Yup. We have to stop." He rolled back on his heels when I tried to reach for him. "Or else we're going to go too far and we're outside in the open."

He stood and held a hand out for me. "Come on. Let's go get some food."

"Why aren't I as weak or starving as I was yesterday?"

"Yesterday you nearly fully drained yourself before you started pulling from me and the pack. This time, you pulled equally. Plus, you weren't trying to talk to someone so far away through a mate bond. You had a physical grip on Meredith. It made things easier."

"I guess that makes sense."

"But I'm still hungry, which means you are, too. Come on, *cherie.*"

I took in the sight of him as he held out his hand. He was over a foot taller than my five feet plus a few and ripped. Without his shirt on, I had a delicious view of his sculpted abs. His arms were thick and chorded with muscle. I loved how his hair had grown out in the past few weeks, long enough for him to tuck it behind his ears.

He was everything I wanted. "You sure you want me forever?" I asked. I opened myself to the bond so I could feel what he was feeling.

"Absolutely." No hesitation or question.

My heart stuttered at how happy he made me. "Okay." I breathed deep. "Okay."

I took his hand, but he didn't pull me up. "What?"

"And you? Are you sure you want me?"

I bit my lip to try and stop the smile that spread across my face. "For as long as you want me."

"Forever then," he said as he pulled me to my feet.

"Okay. Forever." I stood on my tip-toes and pressed a quick kiss to his lips.

He said something in French.

"I don't know what that means."

He laughed again, not telling me.

Damn it. That meant I was going to have to learn the language.

"Now, let's really go get some food."

"Okay." I would've agreed to anything he said in that moment, with those dimples in his cheeks and love in his eyes.

He pressed his forehead against mine. "Thank you."

"For what?"

"For being you." He sighed in a huge dramatic way as he stared down at me. "This is good. We're good."

I cupped his cheek with my hand. "Are you okay?"

"I am now."

"And before?"

"I was worried. We had the full moon coming in a couple of days and the Tribunal after that. We didn't have time to get you used to the idea of being a wolf and you were so scared. I didn't want to push you."

"I'm sorry."

"No. Don't be. This is a good day. For the first time since I bit you, I feel like we're going to be okay."

I thought about it for a second. It was like a huge weight had been lifted that I didn't even know I was carrying. "Me, too."

I ran my fingers through his hair. My heart was full. So full, I didn't know it was possible to be so happy. So in love.

He pressed one more kiss to my lips, and then to my forehead, before grabbing my hand in his. "Ready?"

"Yeah." And I was. For anything. With him.

Chapter Sixteen

By the time we got back to the cafeteria, I was dying with hunger. The witchy-wolfy stuff had used up a ton of energy. Add in the wolf playtime and the long walk back, and I was a million calories into the red. For once, everyone was busy when I stepped through the doors. There were no more stares, mean looks or questioning glances.

Saving one of our own had drained everyone, but the pack felt whole. Healed. And I finally felt like a member of it.

The people who weren't in our pack only added to the feeling. It was nice being around so many wolves. I wouldn't want it every day, but for now, it felt good. Happy.

Everyone was chowing down. The cooks were even grabbing bites in between filling orders. I'd wiped everyone out, but all-in-all it had turned out well. Almost everyone wore some sort of sweatpants or hoodie. Some guys opted for no shirt, but the girls didn't seem to be complaining.

I'd asked Dastien on our walk back how the stashes of clothes got replenished, and he grabbed the backpack. Apparently there were bins filled with backpacks of clothing, water, protein bars, and first aid kits stashed around the woods. Everyone had to replace what they took. Not a bad system. We'd go back tomorrow and return the cleaned sweats.

"I'm going to grab us some food," Dastien said.

"Cool," I said, and continued to our usual table.

Someone shrieked in my ear just before arms squeezed all the breath from my lungs. I laughed and leaned into Meredith.

"Thank you. I don't know what I'd do without you," she said.

I spun. "You scared the crap out of me." I shook her a few times. "I was about to promise to join the coven to save you!"

She pulled back, eyes wide. "You didn't. You didn't do that, did you?"

"Chill, chica. No, I didn't. But I was seriously considering doing it, until Luciana gave away what would break the curse." I shook my head. "You're looking much better." And she was. Her skin was nearly back to its normal color. Her eyes were still a little sunken and she was too thin, but that would change.

"I'm feeling much better. I've been eating nonstop since you took off."

"How long were we gone?"

"Three hours."

"Holy shit. No wonder I'm starving. I'm pretty sure my stomach has already eaten itself."

Donovan and Dastien came back with two trays each. I rubbed my hands together as we sat down. "Let's do this whole werewolf eating thing."

Meredith laughed. "I told you you'd like it."

When I first got to St. Ailbe's, keeping up with the werewolf metabolism had been a real pain in my butt. I could never seem to eat enough, which I'd found endlessly irritating. I still wasn't eating enough, but I was getting better at it. Slowly, but surely.

Chris and Adrian sat at our usual table. So did Shannon. I gave her a nod, and she nodded back. We weren't best friends, and I wasn't holding my breath for it either, but maybe one day...stranger things had happened.

Donovan put his trays on the table, and pulled me to my feet for a tight hug. "Thank you. I know you didn't understand what I was trying to tell you about the curse, but you tried. And you did well."

"Not at first."

"You didn't give up. And that's what's important." He paused. "You've found yourself a good mate."

I blushed. "Um, thanks?" I said when he didn't release me.

Donovan laughed, squeezing me tighter. "I was sayin' that to Dastien."

I laughed. "Right."

"Get your own mate, Dono," Dastien said.

"I did." Donovan shot Meredith a look that was so strong, it made me blush. I couldn't stop the stupid grin that spread across my face even if I tried.

I spotted Meredith's family at the next table. Meredith's mom was gushing to her dad about what a powerful mate their daughter had.

I raised an eyebrow at Donovan and he winked back.

Good thing he was taking that in stride.

I waved at Meredith's family.

"Thank you," Max said.

"This time, I'll accept it."

As I turned back to my ginormous mountain of food, I couldn't help but think of my first meals at St. Ailbe's and how much had changed over past two months. It wasn't always easy, but it was good. Especially Dastien. I peeked at him. How could he be so appealing just sitting there?

Dastien leaned over, brushing my hair away from my face. The look in his eyes told me he knew what I was thinking. "Eat, *cherie*. Then we can be alone again."

The way he said "alone" sent shivers down my spine.

"So, girly," Meredith said. "You've got the full moon and your birthday in two days. How are we celebrating?"

Everyone at the table stopped eating to look at me. Great. Just when I was done with the staring.

"Um, actually, Dastien accidentally spilled the beans about going to see Paul van Dyk next Saturday."

"I don't know that trance is their kind of music," Dastien said.

"Hey. I love dancing," Meredith said. "I don't really care what kind of music it is."

"Well, that's what we're doing. And I was hoping to go shopping before."

Meredith clapped her hands. "And I love shopping."

I laughed. "So we've got a plan?"

"Only totally."

"Good. Can I eat now?"

"I guess. It's just I've been out of it for days, and I feel like I've missed so much." She continued to talk. It was good to see her back to her usual self.

"*A ghrá*, let the lass eat," Donovan said with a laugh.

Meredith poked Donovan with her fork. "Shut it, you. I accepted you a few hours ago and you're already trying to boss me around." She poked him again.

"Enough with the fork, you crazy girl."

I grinned at them. "They're kind of adorable, right?"

Dastien raised an eyebrow. "You want me to agree that Donovan is adorable?"

I pressed a kiss to his cheek.

He placed his hand on my knee and squeezed it gently. *I do think they're pretty cute.*

I jerked away from him for a second. "Did you just talk? In my head?" I whispered.

He grinned, showing his dimples. *I love you, cherie.*

"Say it again."

He pressed his mouth by my ear. "I love you." He kissed my cheek. "Now eat. I can feel your hunger, and it's making me even more hungry."

I laughed. "Okay." I took a bite of pot roast and moaned.

This got me a double eyebrow raise from Dastien. *Now, if only I could get you to make that noise when we're alone.*

My face couldn't have burned brighter.

"Why's your face so red?" Meredith asked.

I pushed my tray away and thumped my head on the table. "No reason." My voice was muffled but I knew she'd hear it.

"You're doing that thing, aren't you?" Chris said.

"What thing?" Adrian asked.

"The talk in each other's head thing."

I sat up to see him shaking his head.

"You're going to be even more impossible to watch now, aren't you?" Shannon said.

I shot her a look and she had the grace to say a quick apology.

"I told you you'd be able to do it," Meredith said. "Hey, why can't we do that?"

Donovan muttered something in a language I'd never heard before. Probably Irish. He looked up at the ceiling and laughed.

Meredith elbowed him and he laughed harder. When she went to elbow him again, he caught it. "No. You're misunderstanding me. I'm not laughing at you. I'm happy." He pulled her in for a quick kiss, and Meredith's milky skin turned bright red. "We'll get there when we get there."

This was good. This was the way friends were supposed to be. The way love was supposed to be. Happy.

I sighed. I hoped it stayed this way.

Dastien grasped my free hand. What's wrong?

"The Tribunal. Do you think it's going to be okay?"

"I know it will be. I won't stand for it to be any other way, okay?"

"You can't promise that."

"No. And it might be hard. But we'll get through it, like we've gotten through the rest of it."

I nodded.

"Eat. Enjoy being with our friends. We've got a big couple of days coming up. Filled with fun things. I can't wait." He ran his finger down my cheek.

"Me too."

I love you, he said through our bond.

I love you, too.

Dastien's eyes widened for a second before his dimples showed up. He pressed a kiss to my forehead.

The future was never certain. I knew how quickly life could change, but with Dastien by my side, I somehow believed that everything would be okay. I couldn't predict what was going to happen at the Tribunal, but for the first time, I felt secure in who I was. Not only in who I was, but in who I was with Dastien.

Maybe it was just as easy as Rosa said. If you believed it to be true, it would be.

I grasped Dastien's hand in mine, and felt the love through our bond. All in all, it was a pretty great day.

The story continues in Book 3 of the Alpha Girl Series.
Available October 14, 2015

An all new series from Ink Monster and Aileen Erin.
Available October 14, 2015

Acknowledgments

Thank you to all my readers! I'm so happy with the love for *Becoming Alpha*. I hope you liked *Avoiding Alpha* just as much.

No writer can survive without amazing critique partners. They're the ones who keep you honest, push you to do your best, and encourage you through all the many drafts. It's my firm belief that a good critique partner is worth their weight in gold.

Thank you, Lauren Stone. You're my rock. I got lucky when I was assigned to you as a One. You're officially stuck with me. FOREVER.

Christina Bauer, my partner in crime, thank you for everything you do. We're killing it, girlfriend. So lucky to have found you, and so excited about what's to come.

To Kelly Peterson and Guillian Helm at INscibe Digital—You ladies rock! Thank you for all of your hard work and patience. Ink Monster wouldn't be where it is today without you!

Thank you, Kime Heller-Neal. Your daily emails and encouragement keep me going. Thank you for keeping me honest.

To Mary Karlik—You're encouragement and feedback is priceless. I guess I'll forgive the whole being an Aggie thing. ;)

To my Halcyon Bastards—You each inspire me. Counting down the days till we meet again.

To everyone at Seton Hill University's Writing Popular Fiction program who read my work, gave me feedback, or sat with me in the Marriott lobby and laughed into the wee hours—I wouldn't be writing without you all. I feel lucky and blessed to know each and every one of you. The WPF is a second family that I treasure greatly.

Kristi Latcham—You're an amazing woman. Thank you for catching all of my little errors. I'd be lost without you! Hopefully I didn't make any typos in this acknowledgement section, but I'm not holding my breath!

To my husband, Jeremy—Thank you for always being willing to read pages, even after a long day at work. You're my everything. I cherish all of your feedback and notes, and strive to make you proud. You have my heart.

To the rest of my family—I love you more than words can say. Each and every one of you. There are way too many of you to list out, but you know who you are. Yes, I'm talking to you!

And to any aspiring writers out there, just do it. Read a ton. Write every single day.

"This is how you do it: You sit down at the keyboard and you put one word after another until its done. It's that easy, and that hard." –Neil Gaiman

"Be ruthless about protecting writing days, i.e., do not cave into endless requests to have 'essential' and 'long overdue' meetings on those days." –J.K. Rowling

Aileen Erin is half-Irish, half-Mexican, and 100% nerd--from Star Wars (prequels don't count) to Star Trek (TNG FTW), she reads Quenya and some Sindarin, and has a severe fascination with the supernatural. Aileen has a BS in Radio-TV-Film from the University of Texas at Austin, and an MFA in Writing Popular Fiction from Seton Hill University. She lives with her husband in Los Angeles, and spends her days doing her favorite things: reading books, creating worlds, and kicking ass.

Follow her on Twitter: @aileen_erin
Follow her on Facebook: www.facebook.com/aelatcham